Poopsie Pomerantz, Pick up your feet

It seemed as if Celeste were looking down at her.

Poopsie Pomerantz, Pick up your feet

PATRICIA REILLY GIFF

Illustrated by LESLIE MORRILL

Delacorte Press

Published by
Delacorte Press
Bantam Doubleday Dell Publishing Group, Inc.
666 Fifth Avenue
New York, New York 10103

LIBRARY OF CONGRESS CATALOGING IN PUBLICATION DATA

Giff, Patricia Reilly.
　Poopsie Pomerantz, pick up your feet / Patricia Reilly
Giff; illustrated by Leslie Morrill.
　　　p.　　cm.
　Summary: Poopsie's plans for self-improvement
include losing enough weight to fit into a medium-sized
bathing suit and becoming a prima ballerina.
　ISBN 0-385-29693-2
　[1. Ballet dancing—Fiction.　2. Weight control—
Fiction.]
I. Morrill, Leslie H., ill.　II. Title.
PZ7.G3626Po　1989
[Fic]—dc19　　　　　　　　　　　　88-15478
　　　　　　　　　　　　　　　　　　CIP
　　　　　　　　　　　　　　　　　　AC

Manufactured in the United States of America

March 1989

10 9 8 7 6 5 4 3 2 1

BG

With love
to Anne Reilly Eisele,
my sister, my friend

Special thanks to the ballet stars
of Naquag School, Rutland, Massachusetts,
who shared their time and experiences with me . . .

and to Janet Chase of Poway, California,
who danced to show me how.

Poopsie Pomerantz, Pick up your feet

1

"That's enough, Tracy," Poopsie Pomerantz yelled, "I'm spinning around like crazy." Peeking from under the blindfold, she looked for the donkey picture tacked to the wall.

It was nowhere in sight.

Tracy Matson grabbed her shoulders and gave her another spin.

"Stop. I have to sneeze."

"Yuck-o," Tracy said. "It's a good thing you're the last one with that kerchief. Sneezing all over the place every two minutes."

Poopsie drew in her breath and sniffed. "A person can't help it if she has allergies."

Tracy snorted. She gave Poopsie one last twirl and a little shove. "Giddyap."

"Yeow." Poopsie took a couple of running steps, then reached out to stop herself.

"Stay away from me with that pin," someone said, sliding away from her. Whoever it was had a mouthful of potato chips. Probably Richard. He hadn't stopped eating since her party had started. There wouldn't be a single potato chip left for her.

Poopsie wiggled her nose until the blindfold slid down a little. She could just about see a corner of the striped couch, the tan lamp, and on the table a picture of her little brother, Teddy, in his birthday suit.

Good grief. She had forgotten about that picture. She brushed past it, turning it around quickly so no one would notice. What was the matter with her mother anyway, leaving a thing like that hanging around?

"Stop peeking," Tracy said.

"I'm not." Where was that donkey? Poopsie stepped over Leroy Wilson's foot, then veered in the opposite direction.

"So what if she cheats?" Richard said, arms in the air. "She can't get the prize anyway. It's her party."

Poopsie reached out and stabbed the donkey tail into the paper. "I can so win. It's my birthday. I can do what I want."

Mrs. Pomerantz popped her head into the room and looked at the donkey picture. "Whose pin is the red one?"

Tracy raised one finger. "Mine, of course."

Mrs. Pomerantz squinted at the donkey tails. "I think red's the closest."

"I don't," Poopsie said under her breath.

"Dumb game." Richard stuffed another handful of potato chips into his mouth. "When do we get to eat the cake?"

"What's the prize?" Tracy cut in.

"A book," said Mrs. Pomerantz. She turned Teddy's picture around again on her way back to the kitchen.

"A book?" Tracy wrinkled her nose. "Your idea, Poopsie?"

"Uh-uh." Poopsie crossed her fingers. "My mother's." She remembered spotting it in the mall last week, a skinny book with fat green letters: *Put On Your Own Magic Show.* Inside, the first picture showed a beautiful girl with a magic wand. Poopsie could just see herself with that wand, twirling it around, doing a thousand tricks. Everyone in High Flats would stand there watching, they'd be crazy to find out how she . . .

". . . staring at nothing . . . your mouth open . . . waiting for a fly to zoom right in," Tracy was saying.

Poopsie jumped. She reached under the couch and pulled out a flat package.

Ripping off the paper, Tracy glanced down at the book, then threw it on the table. "Where do you think I can find a midget to put on the show?"

Everyone stared at her.

3

"The book," Tracy said impatiently. *"Put On Your Own Midget Show.* Where do you think—"

Richard leaned over. "Magic, dumbo. Not midget." He and Leroy started to laugh, slapping each other on the back, pointing at her.

"Pair of idiots," Tracy said. "I wouldn't be so quick to laugh . . . especially you, Richard, showing off your teeth like that. I bet you haven't brushed those fangs since school closed for the summer." She turned to Leroy. "And you, wearing that football helmet all over the place. I bet you even sleep in it."

Poopsie glanced at the boys. Richard was chomping down on a potato chip, not one bit bothered about his teeth. Tracy was right. They were a mess, yellow as butter, with chipped edges. Leroy was grinning. He tapped the top of his green Jets helmet. "Going to be a football player. Professional." He grabbed Richard's head in an arm lock and they slid off the couch, Richard spitting bits of potato chips all over the place. Disgusting.

"How about it's time for me to open my birthday presents?" she asked, still thinking about that magic book. Wouldn't you know someone like Tracy Matson would win it? If only her donkey pin had been a half inch closer. She had the world's worst luck.

She cleared her throat. "Yes, I think I'll open my presents."

Nobody was paying attention. Leroy and Richard

were digging into the potato chips now, fighting for the last big one, still laughing, and Tracy, her face red, sat on the couch, her arms folded, her lower lip stuck out, staring at them.

No, no one was paying attention. Who wanted to pay attention to the youngest, shortest, fattest kid in High Flats? Poopsie looked over at Teddy's picture . . . not the youngest anymore, anyway.

"That's it then." Poopsie reached for the top package. "This is from my grandmother. She always sends the best stuff." Too bad her grandmother didn't know she was into magic or, better still, ballet.

She tore open the package. "Just what I needed, a bathing suit." She held it up, showing off the white knitted suit with purple elephants running all over it. She couldn't help noticing the tag sticking out the back: L for large.

It certainly looked large.

Tracy snickered. "Perfect for a little elephant."

Something else was in the box. A small notebook: *Wish Book*. Poopsie held it up. "Neat."

"I could fill that up in about half a minute with wishes for you," Tracy said. "Lose a little weight, stop being such a Lily Liver all the time, afraid of everything. Stop . . ."

Poopsie swallowed, trying not to pay attention to Tracy. She'd start right in after the party and write her wishes down in her best handwriting.

She reached for the next package. Tracy's. It was wrapped in red-and-green Christmas paper.

"Crazy," Leroy said. "It's the middle of the summer."

"All I could find, Leroy," Tracy said. "It's what's inside that counts."

Poopsie looked down. What was inside were four boxes of M & M's. The boxes had been opened, then closed again. Poopsie shook them. It sounded as if about six M & M's were left in each one.

"Time to eat," Mrs. Pomerantz called from the door.

"Just a minute," Poopsie said. "I have two more presents here."

"Open them later," Richard said.

"Good idea," her mother said. "If Teddy wakes up, he'll be all over the place."

Poopsie sighed. Everyone thought having a baby brother was terrific . . . everyone cooing and gitchy-gooing over him. The truth was, Teddy had turned out to be a pest, a sticky wet pest. "All right, I'll just take my presents with me." She scooped them up and led the way into the dining room.

Her mother had fixed up the whole place. The table was set with a pink cloth and blue paper plates. A bunch of yellow streamers looped down from the light fixture.

Tracy looked up. "You can hardly see with this stuff hanging all over the place."

"Looks neat, doesn't it?" Poopsie said.

"Cut the cake," said Richard. "I've got to get out of here."

"Me too," said Leroy. "Football practice."

Poopsie held up her hands. "Wait a second. We haven't sung 'Happy Birthday' to me yet, and I want to open these presents."

Richard looked up at the ceiling. "If you think I'm going to sing that crazy . . ."

Just then her mother appeared with the cake. It was the Coca-Cola kind with mint icing.

Tracy leaned forward. "Is that green?"

Poopsie nodded, mouth watering. It was her favorite.

"I thought we were getting chocolate," Richard said. "Everyone gets chocolate. I came all the way over here . . ."

Poopsie's mother began to sing. "Happy birthday to you . . ."

Poopsie sang too—loud. Her mother always said she had a very nice voice. Besides, Richard wasn't singing, and neither was Leroy.

"Make a wish," said her mother.

Poopsie closed her eyes. She didn't have to think twice. "Ballet lessons," she said under her breath, her lips hardly moving. That would be the first on her list in the new book.

She took a deep breath and blew out the candles . . . all except one.

"Forget that wish," said Tracy. "You're out of luck."

Poopsie grabbed the knife. "I still get another one."
She dug the knife into the cake: "Ballet lessons . . .
ballet lessons," thinking, Please, please, as her mother
took the knife to cut thick slices for them.

"Doesn't work so well for a wish," Tracy said. "You
can't mess up just cutting a cake. Know what I mean?"

"No," Poopsie said, but she knew Tracy was right.
Last year she had wished for a horse, and that certainly
hadn't happened. Her mother wouldn't even let her
get a bowl of fish.

She cut the icing off her slice to save for last, then
shoved a hunk of cake in her mouth and tore open
Richard's present. "Nice," she muttered, thinking she
might have known. A model plane, gray plastic with
about a thousand directions. The last thing in the world
she wanted.

"Now yours," she told Leroy. She picked up the soft
package with the pale green ribbon.

He gave her a quick smile.

Leroy was the nicest boy she knew, even if he didn't
like birthday parties and he didn't sing "Happy Birthday."

"You pick it out?" she asked.

"Nah." He shook his head. "My mother."

Poopsie tore into the wrapping. Inside was a pale
green leotard. Beautiful.

Leroy's mother must know she was dying for ballet
lessons.

"You pick it out?" Poopsie asked.

Just then Teddy appeared at the door, his diaper trailing.

Tracy held her fingers up to her nose.

"Ma," Poopsie yelled, closing her eyes.

Richard stuffed the last piece of cake in his mouth and stood up. "Time to go."

"Me too," said Leroy.

Tracy leaned over and scooped up a piece of icing from the cake plate. "I think I'll do a little fishing." She yanked on a streamer. "I'll pick up my book on the way out."

Poopsie followed her. "If you don't want the book, we could swap."

"Swap what?"

Poopsie rubbed the back of her hand on her mouth. "Uh, the model plane?"

"Are you crazy?"

"How about the M & M's? You love M & M's."

"I'm a little sick of them right now." Tracy tucked the book under her arm and went out the door after the boys.

Poopsie stood there looking after them. She was glad they were leaving.

She had to blow her nose.

It would be nice to do it without Tracy carrying on about it all over the place. Besides, there was a piece of cake left. She wanted to grab it before her mother put it in the refrigerator for supper.

WISH BOOK

Poopsie Pomerantz

I Wish I Were:

a ballerina...the star kind.

I Wish I Had:

Bathing suit - Size M.

If I Had a Hundred Dollars I'd:

Get a horse.

2

It was almost time to get up. Poopsie opened her eyes and looked at the picture of the ballerina taped to her mirror. The dancer stood high on her toes, her arms curved over her head, her silver leotard sparkling.

Poopsie had named her Celeste, her own name, the name almost no one ever called her. She stretched, wondering why she was nicknamed Poopsie. Something from when she was a baby, probably, something horrible. She wouldn't even ask.

When she looked at Celeste she could almost see her dancing, almost hear the music. If only she could dance like that.

In the next room Teddy was banging something against the side of his crib, babbling to himself. Poopsie heaved herself up and listened to the sounds of her parents down in the kitchen, first her mother's light voice, then the rumble of her father's. A moment later the tea kettle began to whistle.

She slid her legs over the side of the bed, grabbed her Sleeping Beauty robe, and took the stairs two at a time down to the kitchen.

Her father looked up from his newspaper. "You always know when the toast is ready," he said, patting the seat next to him.

Poopsie slid onto the chair and reached for the jelly. "Listen. I have to take ballet lessons. Don't say no again. Please." She stopped for a breath. "I've got this terrific green leotard and everything."

Her mother sighed. "Teddy's going to need a winter snowsuit." She leaned over. "And maybe you'll need braces. Those front teeth look a little . . ." She closed her eyes. "The hot-water heater is probably going to go any minute."

"Lessons don't cost that much," Poopsie said. "Besides, when I get to be famous I'll pay it all back."

Her father grinned. Then he shook his head. "Maybe next year. You'll be older. Right now they're laying off a lot of men down at Blue Seal Tile. We've got to save our money for a rainy day."

Her mother broke in. "Why do you have to have ballet lessons anyway?"

Poopsie thought of Celeste on her mirror, Celeste with the skinny legs and the pale nose. A person like

Poopsie headed for the kitchen.

Celeste wouldn't know what it was like to have jiggly thighs and a nose that was red around the edges.

Tracy Matson wouldn't fool around with someone like that. She wouldn't call her a baby all the time, boss her around. . . .

Poopsie raised one shoulder. "Ballet is important stuff."

Her mother smiled. "So is breakfast. Have some cereal."

Poopsie shook her head. "Too hot." She took a bite of toast, and then another.

"Then just warm up a bottle for Teddy. He's going to be screaming any minute."

"That kid's such a pain," Poopsie said. "Why does he need a snowsuit anyway? We can just pile the blankets on top of his carriage . . ."

"Poopsie. Get the bottle, will you?"

Poopsie stood up and opened the refrigerator door to reach for the milk. "I've got to have lessons. I've been waiting since I was about five years old." She went over to the stove with it.

"Not the stove," her father said. "Warm it under the faucet."

"Everybody thinks I'm a baby around here." Poopsie blasted the water over the bottle. "Can't take ballet lessons. Can't warm the milk on the stove . . ."

"Take it upstairs," her mother said, pushing back her chair. "Then play with him a little while. Try to keep him quiet while I finish up down here."

Poopsie started up the stairs, banging into each step. "I want to go swimming. I'm hot. I'm dying. It's about a hundred degrees in here."

"Two minutes," her mother said. "As soon as I finish in the kitchen."

Poopsie dropped the bottle into the crib and looked at Teddy. He was drooling all over the place, and he was wet. Maybe worse than wet.

"I can't stand it in here," she yelled down. "The whole bedroom smells."

"Poopsie," her mother said. "I don't want to hear another word. Not one more word."

Poopsie slid down on the floor.

After a moment Teddy leaned over the side of the crib. He was holding his bottle in one hand, the milk dripping out of it onto the floor. "Shoom," he said.

"What does that mean?" Poopsie turned the bottle right side up in his hands. She felt mean inside, terrible. She was never going to get ballet lessons. She was never even going to get out of the house to go swimming. She felt like dying of the heat.

She heard the front door close behind her father. In the kitchen her mother began to rattle the plates around. Teddy kept gurgling.

It seemed like forever before she came upstairs. "Whew," she told Teddy, kissing the top of his head. "Do you need a bath."

"About ballet," Poopsie began.

"It's a hundred degrees in here," her mother said. "Give me a break. I can't even think straight."

"Can I go swimming now?"

"Yes. Go. Make your bed first."

Poopsie went into her bedroom. She pulled the spread over the sheets and reached for her elephant bathing suit. Even though it said large, it was tight, very tight.

She took a breath. She couldn't wait to jump in the river. She ran downstairs, raced into the kitchen for a fistful of vanilla cookies, then banged open the screen door. The old inner tube was standing on the porch. She grabbed it and started down High Flats Road, stuffing the cookies into her mouth.

Halfway to the bridge, someone called her. Mrs. Clausson. Good grief. She'd never get in the water.

"Poopsie? Do me a favor?"

Poopsie sighed. She lay the tube down at the edge of the dusty road and went toward Mrs. Clausson's boardinghouse. "Hot," she said.

Mrs. Clausson wiped her forehead. "A little. I try not to notice these things. I just put a vision of ice cubes up in my head and I feel cool."

"Vision?" Poopsie asked.

"You know, something you see up in your head."

"Oh."

"Anyway, in the hot weather I picture ice cubes. When it's freezing out I think of frying pans."

"Really?" Poopsie had a vision of her bathing suit, a

little skinny one. She tried to vision herself little and skinny too.

It didn't work. All that came out was a plump-o Poopsie in a too-tight elephant bathing suit.

"How about stopping at Mrs. Wilson's," Mrs. Clausson asked, "and drop off this recipe? It's my best one for squid. Mrs. Wilson can't wait to try it."

"Sure," Poopsie said.

Mrs. Clausson wiped her forehead again. "It's back to school soon, right?"

"Right." Poopsie reached up with one bare foot to scratch the side of her leg. She hoped Mrs. Clausson wasn't going to keep her there all morning talking about crazy stuff like visions and back to school.

"Loved school," Mrs. Clausson said. "That's where I got the vision idea. My third-grade teacher told me about it. 'Put your vision right up there in colored chalk, boys and girls. Then it'll happen. Sure as the sun comes up over the bridge every morning and disappears down the other side every night—' " Mrs. Clausson broke off. "What was her name?"

"Uh . . . who?"

Mrs. Clausson waved her hand. "My third-grade teacher. Never mind." She handed Poopsie the recipe. "Just . . ."

"I know. Give it to Leroy's mother."

Poopsie backed down Mrs. Clausson's front path, picked up the inner tube, and started for Mrs. Wilson's.

She took a quick look at the recipe, wondering what Leroy was going to get for supper tonight.

She had never heard of squid. Maybe it was some kind of cold pudding or Jell-O. That's all her mother had made for dessert since this heat wave had started.

"Remove arms by cutting from the head," Poopsie read.

She stopped dead in the middle of the road. That didn't sound like dessert, at least she hoped not. Cutting from the head . . . not off the head . . . Did that mean the poor thing's arms were stuck on the head somehow?

She couldn't believe that Mrs. Wilson was dying to cook something like that.

She certainly couldn't believe that Leroy was going to eat it.

And there was Leroy. He was standing in his front path, his green Jets football helmet jammed down over his head, whacking a baseball with a rusty golf club. "You see an orange golf ball lying around?" he asked.

"Sorry," she said, shaking her head. "Listen, will you give this recipe to your mother? From Mrs. Clausson."

Leroy gave the ball another whack. "She's got the worst recipes in the world."

"I guess so," said Poopsie.

"What is it now?"

Poopsie raised her shoulder. "I really don't know exactly."

Leroy reached for the recipe and put it down on the path, aiming the golf club at it. "I think this is going to get lost."

"I've got to get into the water, Leroy," Poopsie said. "Right now."

"I wish Richard would hurry up," Leroy said. "We're going fishing. Going to take the old rowboat down and catch a pickerel or something."

"Great," Poopsie said. There probably wasn't a fish from this end of the river to Hancock, the water was so warm.

She hoisted the inner tube over one shoulder and raced the rest of the way to the water.

Tracy Matson was there already, up on the bridge, dangling her legs over the side. Poopsie waved to her, then rolled the inner tube into the river and tried to jump on top of it.

"Missed," she told herself as she went down. She always seemed to do something dumb like that when Tracy was around.

She stayed under as long as she could, the icy river numbing her arms and legs, feeling cool for the first time all day. When she felt as if her lungs would burst, she kicked down to the bottom, dug her toes in the mud, and shot up again.

Then she remembered. Her plan for asking her mother and father about the ballet lessons hadn't worked, hadn't worked at all. She was out of luck. Then she thought of Mrs. Clausson and her third-grade teacher. She wondered if that vision stuff worked. Maybe she could give it a try. It was really her only chance.

WISH BOOK

Poopsie Pomerantz

I'd Give Fifty Cents If:

Visions could work.

3

It was September, the week before school started, a horrible time for allergies. Poopsie's nose was red, she couldn't stop sneezing, and she had nothing to do. It probably wasn't so bad that she was going back to school, even if she was getting Mrs. Fixx, the strictest teacher in the whole world.

She walked down to Tracy's house. "You there?" she shouted.

Nobody answered.

"Tracy," she yelled as loud as she could. Maybe Tracy was in the bathroom or something and couldn't hear her. "Tra-cy."

Tracy stuck her head out the bedroom window. "Don't I get one minute of peace around here? Yelling and shouting like that. I'm busy."

"What are you doing?"

"Can't talk about it now. Go away."

Poopsie wandered down the street. Leroy and Richard were fishing somewhere again. She had seen the top of Leroy's Jets helmet as they raced their bicycles down the path to the river.

Leroy must be in love with that helmet.

She looked around for a place to sit, somewhere with a patch of shade. It was time to start the vision. She scrunched down under Mrs. Wilson's maple tree, shoved a couple of ants out of the way with a leaf, and leaned back against the trunk.

"Vi-sion," she whispered. "Viii-shin." She drew out the word until it hissed like that skinny old water snake she had almost stepped on this morning, stepped on with her bare feet.

Closing her eyes, she tried to picture a blackboard right in back of her forehead, inside her brain somewhere. "I have a vision of myself," she said. "A vision of walking on my toes." She squeezed her eyes closed tighter, shutting out the sun, thinking about being grown up, and gorgeous, the best ballet dancer in High Flats . . . no, in the world.

"Yes," she'd tell everyone who came to see her. "I nearly didn't get ballet lessons. We were poor, so poor we had to eat squid arms for dinner. I had to vision being a ballerina until I finally got to the stage."

Tracy Matson wouldn't dare call her a baby or Lily Liver again. She'd be much too important for that.

She tried to see herself on the blackboard just the way Mrs. Clausson had said, looking beautiful, looking like the ballerina on the mirror.

She clicked her teeth. All she could see was herself, brown eyes, fat cheeks, and a round stomach with a belly button that stuck right out through the pale green leotard.

Disgusting.

She tried to erase that part out of her vision. She'd have a nice flat belly button that nobody could see.

In her mind she moved down to her legs. Legs with two scabs from falling on the rocks down by the bridge.

Her feet . . . and then the important part of her vision . . . toes.

"Viii-shin," she said again. "A vision of me. I'm up on my toes. I'm strengthening every single toe I've got, every bone."

A pebble hit the tree above her. "The major bone you're strengthening is the one in your head," Tracy Matson said, tossing another stone at a top branch.

Poopsie reached for the toilet paper she had stuck in her shorts pocket. "My allergies are terrible today. My mother says it's from all that goldenrod blowing around."

Tracy made a gagging noise. She marched past carrying a basket. An old blue blanket wrapped around her waist was trailing off into the dust.

Poopsie stood up to follow her, trying to walk on her toes. She held out her arms to keep her balance, and spread her fingers the way she had seen a ballerina do in a movie. "What are you doing with that blanket? Where are you going?"

"Going to China, going to India. Is it any of your business?"

"Slow down," Poopsie begged. "My toes are going to break off right at the knuckles."

Tracy stopped moving. "What are you trying to do, Poopsie? You look like the dunce of the world."

"I'm a dancer," she said.

Tracy snorted.

Poopsie reached for the toilet paper again and took a swipe at her nose. "Aren't you hot carrying that heavy blanket around?"

Tracy didn't answer. "Where did that dog get to?" She shaded her eyes with her fist. "Rebel," she screeched at the top of her lungs. "He's never around when I want him for something. But just bring out a plate of meat and he's right there slobbering all over the place, dying to shovel it all in."

"Then why don't you get . . ." Poopsie began.

"Get what?"

"Some meat. Put it in a plate, wave it around, and maybe . . ."

"Don't be silly, Poopsie. You think I've got all day for that kind of stuff." She cupped her hands around her mouth. "R-e-b-e-l."

Poopsie sank down at the side of the road and pulled

off one sneaker. Her toes were pulsing. "A vision," she told herself without moving her lips.

"R-e-b . . ." Tracy yelled.

"He's right behind you." Poopsie pointed with her sneaker at the dog, who was lumbering up the road toward them.

Tracy crouched down in the middle of the road, snapping her fingers. "Nice dog, nice old . . ." She broke off. "Good grief. Where've you been?" She sniffed a little. "Near miss with a skunk, I see."

Leaning over him, she pointed to the ground. "Lie down." Rebel brushed his tail slowly in the dust, rolling his eyes toward home.

"Come on, Reb," Tracy said in a crooning voice. "This is important stuff."

"Viii-shin," Poopsie muttered, watching Rebel as he sank down, panting. She pulled off the other sneaker and looked at her sock. There was a hole in the toe.

She held her foot by one ankle and looked to see if her big toe was red. It certainly felt red. It felt hot. It felt as if it would never be able to spend the day walking around on the tip.

"Now," said Tracy. "This is the beginning." She whipped the blanket over the dog. "Don't move. Stay right there."

"What are you doing?" Poopsie asked.

Tracy twirled around. "You still here? Spying on my private business?" Then she grinned. "As a matter of fact, you'd better stick around. You might see something interesting."

Poopsie lowered her foot and wiggled her big toe back and forth. "You trying to suffocate your own dog?"

"That's ridiculous," Tracy said. "That's the most ridiculous thing I ever heard in my whole life."

The blanket lumped up in the center and began to move slowly down High Flats Road.

Tracy pointed at it. "Stay," she yelled.

The blanket settled down and was still.

Tracy rummaged around in the basket, throwing out an old hat and a couple of knobby paper bags.

"I was going to ask . . ." Poopsie started. "What are you doing anyway?"

"Magic," Tracy cut in. "I'm practicing magic. I'm going to get good at it, really good."

"Really?" Poopsie didn't say anything for a minute. "You mean like in the book I gave you?"

"Exactly."

Poopsie clicked her teeth a little. Exactly her idea when she bought that book.

"Show that idiot Leroy and his friend Ratty Richard a thing or two," Tracy said.

"That dog must be hot under there." Poopsie looked down. "My mother said you're supposed to be careful of things like that. Dogs shouldn't get overheated."

"Only for a minute. He doesn't mind. He loves that blanket. He sleeps on it every single night." Tracy pulled a long thin stick out of the basket and waved it around. "Mag-ic mag-ic pres-ky."

Poopsie leaned forward, watching.

"Disappear," Tracy yelled. She yanked the blanket up in the air.

The dog looked up at her, blinking.

Poopsie started to laugh, then stopped. Tracy was mean as a snake when she was annoyed.

Tracy put her hands on her hips. "I know what's the matter," she said. "I know exactly. We don't have the right kind of magic wand."

"Oh," said Poopsie.

Tracy stood there, fist on her forehead, thinking. "I know. We'll go up to Gypsy Wild—"

"I'm not allowed."

"Straight up to Gypsy Wild," Tracy went on. "We'll pick up a good strong stick, maybe an extra one or two for spare."

"Out, Tracy. That's definitely out. My mother said—"

"Forget I mentioned it." Tracy started to shake the dust from the blanket. "I keep forgetting you're just a little kid."

"I am not, Tracy. I'm not. It's just that . . ." Poopsie broke off. She could picture her mother in the kitchen. "I don't want you up there," she had said. She had said it in her serious voice, quietly, looking almost worried.

That was a long time ago, months, maybe even last summer. She tried to remember. Maybe her mother would change her mind now that she was older. She

"Disappear," Tracy yelled.

swallowed. Her mother would have a fit if she went up there. She'd be in a pack of trouble. But that wasn't even it. It was just that she had promised . . .

Tracy was walking up the road away from her.

"Your boat's probably full of water," Poopsie called. "We'd have to bail it out for a half hour, and then we'd still have to walk about a thousand miles at the other end."

Tracy snapped her fingers at Rebel. "Get on home," she told him. "I have to go somewhere. By myself."

"Come on, Tracy. Let's not do that. My mother—"

"You don't have to come. Stay here, Lily Liver. Play with your little brother or some other baby stuff."

"We can find a stick around here. Sticks are lying around all over the place."

"Not the magic kind. Not the kind where there are kid—" Tracy closed her mouth tight, sucking her lips in between her teeth.

"What?"

"What?" Tracy repeated. "You think I'm going to tell you a bunch of scary stuff when you're such a baby you can't even go two inches in a rowboat down to Gypsy Wild?" She flipped her braid over her shoulder. "Besides, when did your mother tell you not to go up there?"

"I don't know. A long time ago."

"See. That was when you were little, really little, four or five. Doesn't make a peanut's worth of difference now."

"That's what I was thinking, I guess."

"Yeah. I'll tell you all about that scary stuff on the way." She gave Rebel a little push. "Go on, Rebel." She turned back to Poopsie. "You're too big to be afraid."

Poopsie worked her feet back into her sneakers as Tracy started up High Flats Road toward the river.

"I'm coming," Poopsie yelled. "I just want to find out about that scary business before we get going."

Tracy looked back over her shoulder. "If you're coming with me, you'd better get a move on."

Poopsie opened her mouth. Then she closed it again. Tracy would just call her Lily Liver if she kept asking. She followed Tracy down the road, wondering if she should say her mother wanted her for something.

It was too late though. Tracy was already at the bridge, climbing into the boat.

Poopsie slithered down the side of the riverbank, grabbing at the reeds to slow herself down.

"Boat's a mess," Tracy said. She hopped over the seat and reached for the oars.

Poopsie pulled off her sneakers and jumped in behind her. The bottom of the boat was disgusting. A half dozen dead worms sloshed back and forth in an inch of water. She took a breath and crawled around Tracy to the back. At least they didn't have to bail.

"What's the scary stuff anyway?" Poopsie asked before she could stop herself. She knew she shouldn't ask. She knew Tracy would make fun of her. She was too worried to keep her mouth shut though.

Tracy poled one of the oars into the mud to push the

boat off, then began to row, the oars biting cleanly into the water. "Kidnappers," she said after a minute.

"Kidnappers," Poopsie repeated. She looked back at the riverbank. It was too far to jump out.

"Nothing to it," Tracy said.

"Are you sure?"

Tracy stuck out her lip, looking irritable. "Are you going to go on about it all day?"

"No, of course not." Poopsie began again slowly. "What's the story anyway?" She tried to sound as if she didn't care. She tried to sound as if kidnappers were just an ordinary thing to her, as if they popped up on High Flats Road every other day or so.

"Don't bother me with that right now," Tracy said. "Look who's coming."

Poopsie glanced up. Leroy was rowing down the river in their direction, along the opposite bank, with Richard in the backseat.

"Want to ram them?" Tracy asked.

Poopsie shook her head. "No thanks. Let me out of here if you're going to start that kind of stuff. My mother says it's very dangerous." If only she were home with her mother right now, having lunch, she thought, or in the backyard.

"What a Lily Liver you are, Poopsie." Tracy sighed. "I'm telling you for your own good. You're afraid of everything that comes down the pike."

Tracy angled the boat toward the opposite side of the river, watching Leroy and Richard out of the corner of her eye. "And your mother is wrong, as a matter of fact. You can swim, can't you? Swim a couple of feet if the boat turns over?"

Poopsie felt her mouth quiver. She brought her hand up and made believe she was rubbing it. Tracy wasn't paying attention though. She dug into the water with the oars. The boat shot forward.

From across the way Leroy saw them coming toward him. "Yeow," he yelled. As fast as he could he headed for the landing on his side.

"Afraid to get your helmet wet?" Tracy shouted. She raced the boat across the river toward him.

Poopsie held on to the sides with both hands. The boat was rocking back and forth, churning up the water. "Let me out of here," she yelled. "I've got to go home."

Tracy rowed faster.

Leroy was pulling hard, nearing the landing rocks.

"Scaredy-cat," Tracy yelled.

Leroy ran his boat up on the rocks. He and Richard jumped out.

Tracy was going too fast to stop. She rammed into a pair of rocks jutting into the water.

"Yeow," Poopsie yelled. She slid off the seat into the wormy water on the bottom of the boat.

Using one oar, Tracy pushed off the rocks. "Get you next time," she told Leroy. "This is war."

Leroy and Richard were dancing around on the

rocks, laughing and pointing as Tracy rowed away from them.

"Don't pay any attention," Tracy said. "Not one bit of attention."

Poopsie looked down. A worm was stuck to her toe. She scrambled back up on the seat and scraped it off with her other foot. "What do you say we go back home? I think it's lunchtime."

Tracy didn't answer. She rowed under the bridge, heading downriver.

"I'm starving," Poopsie said.

Tracy reached into her back pocket with one hand. "Have an M & M or two."

Poopsie looked down at them. The M & M's were damp and pale. They had probably been in Tracy's pocket for weeks. "Where did these come from?"

"Your birth—" Tracy snipped off the word and raised one shoulder. "I don't keep track of little things like that." She raised the oars and let them float past a patch of spiky reeds poking up out of the river.

"Listen, Tracy, about that kidnapper . . ."

"Let's not talk," Tracy said. "Let's concentrate on getting where we're going."

The boat was downstream now, under the trees. They were halfway there. Poopsie dangled her fingers in the river, staring at the rocks and weeds under the clear water, wanting to ask Tracy more. She knew she wouldn't answer though. Sometimes Tracy was mean, really mean.

A school of tiny fish darted past, and then a few inches away a lamprey eel glided by. She shivered and yanked her hand up, glad she wasn't in the water. Those eels could latch on to something and suck the blood right out.

Tracy was watching her.

"Lamper," she said.

Tracy closed her eyes. "You—are—the—biggest—baby," she said, drawing the words out.

Poopsie didn't answer. She watched as they drew closer to the bend of the river, where pine branches hung out over the edge of the water. Her throat felt tight. Tracy was right. She was afraid of everything that came down the pike. She wondered what a pike was. A fish? Down a fish? How could that be? Tracy Matson certainly was strange sometimes.

At the bend Tracy nosed the boat in between two rocks so it would stay wedged in, grabbed a low-hanging branch, and hopped out. Poopsie followed behind her, thinking how much cooler it was here, the light a pale green under the tangle of trees. She had really done it now. In a few minutes, a few steps, she'd be at Gypsy Wild, her promise to her mother broken.

She looked down, following the narrow path behind Tracy. The ground was covered with pine needles, old, brown, and soft under her feet.

"It feels like fall," Tracy said over her shoulder. "I've been sick of this heat, sick of summer. Can't wait for a good snowstorm."

"School," Poopsie said, ducking away from a patch of briars. "It'll be nice."

Tracy snorted. "Don't remind me of that now and ruin a perfectly good day."

"I thought you said—"

"Do you have to ask a thousand questions every two minutes?"

Poopsie pressed her lips together. She wasn't going to say another word, not one word. She counted her steps to make the walk seem faster. Twelve, thirteen, not supposed to be in here, eighteen, nineteen. It was darker now, the pines were taller.

She forgot what number she was up to.

Ahead of her, Tracy had stopped suddenly.

"What's the matter?"

"Nothing. Does something have to be wrong?" Tracy pushed back her red braids. "I'm just checking things out."

Poopsie stood on tiptoe to look over Tracy's shoulder. Ahead was the clearing and the old cabin they called Gypsy Wild. Half falling down, unpainted, it belonged to a family that never came there on vacation anymore.

"I don't want to scare you," Tracy said, "but this is where I think the kidnapper was."

"Uh-uh, Tracy." Poopsie shook her head. "Don't start something like that."

Of course her mother would make her promise not to go there, of course.

"Was, I said. Not now."

37

"How do you know?"

Tracy raised one shoulder. "Lights, a couple of months ago. Candles. My father went up to check it out."

Poopsie's mouth was dry, her tongue stuck to the back of her teeth.

"My father said someone had been in the cabin."

"Maybe not a kidnapper."

"Maybe not," said Tracy. "Then why was he telling my mother about it in a whisper? He didn't want me to hear."

"Let's get out of here."

"I told you it was a long time back," Tracy said and looked down at the ground. "Hey, see there? Dead branches pointing?"

Poopsie rubbed one foot against her leg. "Pointing?" She looked closer. Branches had been broken off a laurel bush. They lay in a circle around the front of the house, the leaves still green and fresh.

"What is it?" Poopsie asked.

Tracy didn't answer. She was bent over, looking at something else on the ground.

"What . . ." Poopsie began again.

"I'm not sure." Tracy picked up a stick. "There's something on it . . . sticky, red. . . ."

"Paint."

Tracy looked at her. "Maybe."

Poopsie touched it with her fingers. "It's wet."

"Kidnapper," Tracy whispered. "He's still here."

Poopsie dashed after Tracy.

"Tracy!" Poopsie wanted to scream.

"They don't like to tell kids," Tracy said.

"It's late." Poopsie looked back toward the boat. "I think we should go back now. Grab a stick and just go back."

"They just tell a little bit. A little bit like 'Don't talk to strangers.' Stuff like that."

Poopsie swallowed. Her mother did say that. She said it all the time. "Are you afraid?" she asked Tracy.

"I'm not afraid of anything," Tracy said, almost whispering. She bit at her lip. "Not afraid of one blessed thing." She grabbed a few branches.

Poopsie opened her mouth. She wanted to say that the branches were too skinny. She wanted to say they looked as if they'd break any minute. She didn't though. She didn't want to waste a minute. They had to get out of there fast.

Tracy picked up one more branch. She looked back over her shoulder, then she began to run.

Poopsie dashed after her, through the trees, down the path to the boat, trying to run faster than she ever had before.

WISH BOOK

Poopsie Pomerantz

If I Could Do One Thing Over I'd:

Never go up to Gypsy Wild.

I Wish I Weren't:

A Lily Liver.

5

It was the first day of school. Poopsie took a last bite of Sugar Bits, crammed a couple of cheese crackers in her mouth, then raced upstairs for her loose-leaf notebook.

In her bedroom she stopped to take a quick look in the mirror. Excellent. Well, not excellent exactly, not like Celeste . . . she looked a little plump-o around the middle. But she loved her new stone-washed jeans and the pink-and-green "I'm Ready to Dance" T-shirt.

She loved going back to school too. She was sick of hanging around worrying about kidnappers, having nightmares about them, looking over her shoulder every time she even walked down High Flats Road.

If only she could tell her mother or her father. How could she? She'd be in a pile of trouble. Not only that.

She could picture her mother's face. She'd be so disappointed. "You promised," she'd say.

Poopsie shook her head. She'd just have to pray that the kidnapper, whoever he was, was about a hundred miles away from High Flats by now.

She hurried down the stairs, trying to put Gypsy Wild out of her mind, trying to vision herself as a ballerina, as Celeste. Her father was still at the table, drinking his coffee and reading the front page of the paper. "Ready to go?" he asked.

Poopsie nodded. "The bus comes in a few minutes." She looked around. "Where's Mom?"

"Outside." He turned the page. "She's putting Teddy in the playpen out on the front lawn. She says she's going to clean this house from top to bottom now that you're going back to school."

Poopsie grabbed her brown-paper-bag lunch, lifted it up to her nose, and sniffed. "Peanut butter. Same old stuff."

She started down the hall and stopped. "Mom's leaving Teddy outside all by himself?"

She heard the clink as her father put the coffee cup back in the saucer, then the swish of the page turning.

"Dad?"

"Hmm?"

"Teddy's going to be all alone out there?"

"Alone with the birds and about a thousand toys in the playpen."

Poopsie took a step back into the kitchen. "Isn't that

dangerous? Suppose a kidnapper comes along? Snatches him right out of there?"

Her father looked up over the paper and smiled at her. "It's nice to see that you're thinking about Teddy, worrying about him."

Poopsie traced her fingers on the table. "Maybe Mom could keep him inside."

Her father stood up. "You can't keep everybody in the house all the time." He ruffled her hair as he went past. "That wouldn't make sense."

Poopsie followed him down the hall. Outside she could hear her mother calling, "The bus is stopping at the end of the road."

"Listen," she said to her father as he started up the stairs. "Suppose . . ."

He looked back. "Mom is calling you."

Poopsie went out the screen door. She could see Tracy Matson in a new pair of overalls and Leroy, looking strange without his helmet, wearing stiff jeans.

She walked across the lawn to the playpen. Teddy was hanging over the bars trying to get out. Her mother, hair in her eyes, was trying to interest him in a squeaky toy.

"Listen, Mom. You'd better not leave him out here by himself," Poopsie said.

"Why not?" Her mother looked up at the sky. "It's not supposed to rain until later."

"Suppose a kidnapper comes by?"

"What?"

"Suppose a kidnapper comes by?" Poopsie asked.

"You know . . . someone who takes kids."

"That, Poopsie, is the least of my worries right this minute." Her mother pointed her chin toward the road. "Don't miss the bus, give me a kiss."

Poopsie gave her mother a quick hug, then started down the path. "Watch him. Watch him every minute."

"Don't worry," her mother called after her.

Poopsie raced down High Flats Road, climbed into the bus, and followed Tracy and Leroy to the back.

Leroy stretched out in the last seat.

"Move over," Tracy told him. "You're going to hog all the room."

"Too bad, Tracy," he said. "This is Richard's seat."

Poopsie slid into the seat in front of Leroy and turned to look out the window. In the aisle, Tracy was furious. "That idiot Richard doesn't even get on until Windsor. How can it be his seat?"

Poopsie's mother had gone into the house already. Poopsie could see Teddy sitting in the corner of the playpen, his back toward the road, rolling a ball back and forth in front of him.

Tracy slammed into the seat next to her. "Sometimes I hate that Leroy."

Poopsie craned her neck to watch Teddy until the bus went around the curve and she couldn't see him anymore. She swallowed, then turned to look at Tracy.

Tracy, head back, had a teaspoon hanging off the end of her nose.

"Dunce," Leroy told her.

46

"A magic trick," she said. "You couldn't do it in a hundred years."

"I wouldn't want to."

Poopsie's father had taught her that trick when she was about six years old, she thought. She stared out the window thinking about kidnappers, and Teddy, and that maybe she could ask the principal if she could call home to find out if Teddy was all right.

The bus slowed down for the Windsor stop. Richard and a few other kids got on, Richard racing to the backseat, pounding Leroy on the head, laughing.

She leaned closer to the window. She could see a drop on the glass, and then another one. They slid down the pane. It was starting to rain. She took a deep breath. Her mother would have to take Teddy in the house now. He was safe. For today anyway.

6

By three o'clock it was pouring. Poopsie jumped off the school bus and started down High Flats Road, hopping in between the puddles, trying not to get her new sneakers wet. She clutched her loose-leaf notebook and her new reader under one arm.

Her mother opened an upstairs window. "Hurry up. You're going to get soaked."

"I don't mind," Poopsie said. She loved the rain. She loved the feel of it on her face, her eyelashes, her nose.

"I have exciting news," called her mother.

"What?"

Her mother laughed and closed the window again.

Licking a drop of rain off her lower lip, Poopsie started to run. She dashed down the driveway, opened the back door with her free hand, and slid into the kitchen.

"In my bedroom," her mother called.

Poopsie ran upstairs, stopped to throw her books on her bed, then went down the hall. Her mother was standing in front of her mirror, leaning forward, a curling iron in her hand.

"What news?" Poopsie stepped over Teddy, who was playing with her mother's slipper in the middle of the rug. "What are you doing?"

Her mother smiled at her in the mirror. "How was the first day?"

Poopsie made a face. "Mrs. Fixx. She says we're going to be camels this year. No water. No bathroom."

"Sounds interesting."

"Matthew Polland was talking and she hung a pink paper tongue around his neck. It had written on it 'I have a long tongue.' And Edward got a snaky thing. It said 'I squirm like a worm in my seat.' "

Her mother laughed. "Do teachers still do that?"

Poopsie shook her head. "Just Mrs. Fixx. She's old. Older than Gram, I think."

"What did you get?"

"A's."

"Terrific." Her mother stood up and twirled around. "How do you like my hair?"

"Puffy."

"Of course it is. This is the first time I've curled it since Teddy was born."

Poopsie sank down on the bed. "Are we going to have a snack? I'm starving."

"You haven't heard my news yet." Her mother reached over and took her slipper out of Teddy's mouth.

"What?"

"You, Poopsie Pomerantz," her mother said, grinning, "are going to have ballet lessons."

Poopsie jumped off the bed.

"Watch out for Teddy."

On one foot, Poopsie stepped around the baby and reached for her mother. "This is it," she said. "I'm going to be famous."

"Of course." Her mother looked serious. "There's a catch though."

Poopsie put her other foot down.

"You'll have to make your own bed . . ."

"That's nothing." Poopsie waved her hand in the air.

"Set the table . . ."

"I'll even do the dishes."

"And baby-sit. I have a job."

Poopsie danced around Teddy. "I'm going to have ballet—" She broke off. "What's the job?"

"Nighttime waitress at the Star Diner, five to ten P.M."

"Terrific. Can we get free hamburgers and stuff?"

"Not quite."

"Wait a minute. At night? When Daddy's on the late shift? After it gets dark? Me and Teddy alone?"

"You haven't heard my news yet,"
Poopsie's mother said.

Her mother looked back at the mirror. She pushed at one side of her hair. "Certainly. You're a big girl now."

Poopsie shivered. "I hate to be alone in the dark."

"Not alone. You'll have Teddy for company."

Poopsie looked at him. He was chomping on the edge of her mother's blue bedspread, eyes half closed. "Some company." She looked out the window. "Suppose there are kidnappers around here? Suppose they find out we're alone in the house? The lock on the back door doesn't even work right."

"I wouldn't worry about that. I'd worry about keeping on the good side of old Mrs. Fixx."

"Tracy says . . ." she began and broke off.

"Tracy," her mother repeated. "I might have known." She opened her dresser drawer. "I don't even have a decent purse to take to work. I'll have to do something about that."

"How long are you going to work?"

"Just until we get ahead a little. Pay for your ballet lessons, Teddy's snowsuit, the hot-water heater. We'll see."

"How do you know for sure that a kidnapper's not around?"

Her mother whirled around and grabbed her, squeezing hard. "Gotcha," she said.

"Really," Poopsie said. "Tell me."

"Really, I think someone is knocking at the back door."

"Let them knock," Poopsie said. "Tell me about the kidnapper."

"Go on," her mother said. "See who it is. It's pouring out there. I don't want someone standing in the rain—" She broke off and opened another drawer.

Poopsie went down the stairs. She could hear banging now. Someone was banging on the door like crazy.

It was Tracy Matson. "Let me in," she shouted. "Want me to drown out here?"

Poopsie opened the door and Tracy rushed in, hair dripping wet, blue T-shirt soaked.

"How'd you get so wet just coming from your house?"

Tracy shook her head. "I've been in the backyard building something. There isn't any room in the garage. Not one inch. My father has his tools, his paint—" She broke off. "Are you having a snack?"

Poopsie looked around the kitchen. "No. Do you want something?"

"What have you got?"

"Bread, I guess." She pulled a bag of white bread from the drawer, took out a slice, and stuffed the crust into her mouth. She passed the bag to Tracy.

"How about muffins?"

"I don't think so," she said, trying to speak clearly.

"I'll take cereal. But hurry. We've got to get down there fast."

Poopsie set the bread on the table and reached for the Sugar Bits in the cabinet. "Down where?"

Tracy went over to the refrigerator and reached in for the milk. "That's what I'm trying to tell you." She grabbed the cereal box from Poopsie and ripped it open.

"Who is it?" her mother called from upstairs.

"Tracy."

"Hi, Tracy," Mrs. Pomerantz called. "Poopsie, come on back and take the baby for a few minutes, will you? I have to go up to the attic. Maybe I have a purse up there."

Tracy tapped Poopsie's shoulder. "Tell your mother you have to take him down to my house. We can't waste any more time around here."

"In the rain?" Poopsie smeared some peanut butter across a slice of bread and tore off the crust. "She'll never let me."

"Poopsie, I mean now," her mother said.

Poopsie stamped up the stairs. She heaved Teddy up. He weighed a ton. "Come on," she said to him, "I'll give you something to eat."

In the kitchen Tracy was finishing the last of her cereal. She had a milk mustache and a dab of peanut butter on her chin.

Poopsie's slice of bread had a small bite out of it. She stared down at it, then lifted Teddy into the high chair and handed it to him.

"How long will your mother be up in that attic?" Tracy asked.

"Who knows?"

"All right. I'm going back. Come down to my house as soon as you can."

Teddy dropped the bread on the floor. It landed peanut-butter side down.

Poopsie leaned over and scooped it up.

He held out his arms, his face a mess of peanut butter.

Tracy pulled him up out of the high chair and set him on the floor. "But what . . ." she began to ask Tracy.

"That kid's disgusting," Tracy said. She held up her fingers. "One. We have to clean out the garage. My father will pay us . . . me fifty cents an hour. I'll split it with you. Twenty cents an hour."

She could save it up, Poopsie thought, pay for some of her ballerina lessons, her mother could stop work sooner. "I'll do it," she said, pulling another slice of bread out of the bag. "Wait a minute. Twenty cents isn't half."

"Don't say a word," Tracy said. "It's my garage, I'm older, I do more work faster."

Poopsie nodded. "I guess so. How many hours do you think it will take?"

"That's not important," Tracy said. "The important thing is . . ." She wiggled her second finger. "We're cleaning the garage for a reason. We don't just care about a clean garage."

"What do you mean?"

"We have to build a box for the magic show. I read all about it in the magic book. You shove someone inside and begin to saw. Everyone thinks you're going to saw the person in half. It turns out she's saved. It's some kind of a trick. I just have to learn the trick."

"Neat." Poopsie looked around. "Where's Teddy?" She raced into the living room. He was rubbing his face into the couch pillow, smearing it with peanut butter.

"Yikes," Poopsie said. She turned the pillow over and walked him back into the kitchen.

"Good thing Leroy gave you that green leotard," Tracy said. "It's a little plain though. I would have liked some spangles and stuff."

Poopsie shook her head. "What are you talking about?"

Tracy grinned at her. "More money for you, Poops. I'm going to charge Leroy and Richard to watch me saw you in half."

"Not me," Poopsie said. "You think I'm going to lie down in some box and let you saw me in half?"

"There you go again, Poopsie. You're afraid of everything." Tracy picked up the peanut-butter jar, took a glob of peanut butter off the side, then set the jar down on a chair. Licking one finger, she opened the back door. "Think of all the money you'll make." She hopped down the three steps to the yard. "Pouring," she yelled.

Poopsie stood at the door for a minute watching the rain smash into the puddles on the driveway. Tracy was zigzagging toward High Flats Road as fast as she could.

She took a breath. She could hear Teddy babbling to himself and her mother moving boxes up in the attic. She thought about being alone in the dark with Teddy.

"All right," she shouted after Tracy. "I'll do it. I need the money."

She bent down to pick up the jar. She wondered how much money she was going to make.

And how fast.

WISH BOOK

Poopsie Pomerantz

If Only:
Time would stop right now.
My mother wouldn't go to
work in two weeks.

7

It was the first Saturday in October. Poopsie stood at the bus stop, her new ballerina shoes in a brown paper bag under her arm. Her mother had taken her to Shoes On Sale for them. They were black, and so soft you could bend them in half. They were also a size too small, but the man didn't have the next size. She kept visioning her feet a size smaller while she waited for the free bus to come over the mountain.

Tracy was standing next to her. She was going to town to buy a bunch of nails for the sawing box. She had borrowed money from Poopsie, the last of her birthday money from Aunt Susan.

A moment later the bus pulled to a stop in front of them. They climbed on and sat in the back.

"Did you go up to Gypsy Wild again?" Poopsie asked.

"Not me," Tracy said.

"Did you hear anything more about a kidnapper?"

Tracy cleaned off the dusty window with the palm of her hand. "Not much . . . well . . . Leroy was telling me there's something up there, something that left fish bones all over the place. A coon, he says, or a beaver. Hah."

"Hah what?"

"Hah, Leroy's got a screw so loose in his head, his brains are looped around his shoulders."

Poopsie leaned closer. "You really think there's a kidnapper up there?"

"I didn't at first," Tracy said, "but now, maybe." She worked on the window a little more. "What's the matter with that bus driver anyway? He's got to be crawling up the mountain. You'd think he was pushing the bus instead of driving."

"What do you think he's doing up there?"

"Driving. I don't know. What are you talking about?"

Poopsie shook her head. "Not the bus driver. The kidnapper."

"What do kidnappers usually do? They wait. They wait for—"

"I hope I'm not going to be late," Poopsie cut in. She could feel her heart pounding. She didn't want to hear what Tracy might say next. She leaned over and peered out the window at the church steeple off to the right and the high school up on the hill. "Almost there."

"I think ballet lessons are a waste of time," Tracy said. "A big waste of time."

Poopsie made believe she didn't hear her.

"You're not the ballet type. You know what I mean?"

Poopsie shook her head.

"You have to be kind of . . . graceful, I guess. You can't be sniffling with allergies all over the place every minute, nose all red. Stuff like that."

Poopsie stood up as the bus came to a stop. "I am so the ballet type, Tracy. You'll see."

She rushed to the front of the bus and hopped off.

As the bus pulled away she could see Tracy shaking her head, talking to herself. Sometimes she wished Tracy would move away. Sometimes she wished she could pay her back the way Leroy and Richard did.

Too bad she was the only other girl in High Flats.

The clock over the First National Bank said 11:06. Poopsie clicked her teeth. Six minutes late already and she still had to get to Main Street. She darted around the corner and ran for two blocks to Ronnie's Restaurant. She stopped a moment until the stitch in her side was gone, then pushed open the door. Miss Adrienne's Theater Ballet was upstairs over the restaurant.

Miss Adrienne must have started already. Poopsie could hear the pom-pom-pom of music and someone counting, one and two and three.

She ran up the stairs two at a time. It sounded as if an elephant were on its way up. She could see a door with glass on the top. She peeked in. About ten girls were lying in a circle, feet in the middle. They were wearing leotards and ballet slippers just like hers. That was all right then. At least she had the right stuff to start.

She looked down at herself. Good grief. She had to change. Where? Nowhere that she could see. She glanced back down the stairs, no one in sight. She began to pull off her sneakers, listening to the music coming from inside. She stood up on her toes to take a look. The girls were raising and lowering their legs, and not one had jiggly thighs.

How was she ever going to take her jeans off and her top without someone coming along? Good thing she had worn her leotard underneath.

She yanked off her jeans, shoes, and socks as fast as she could, watching the stairs. Then she pulled her shirt over her head and stuffed everything in her ballet bag. She toed into her slippers, took a breath, and pushed open the door. She stopped for a moment, took another breath, then tiptoed the rest of the way, sucking in her stomach. She hoped everyone didn't think she looked fat.

Miss Adrienne didn't see her. She was standing on one side, changing a cassette.

Poopsie slid into the circle as quietly as she could. She slipped and landed on someone's arm.

"Ow." The girl gave Poopsie a dirty look and rubbed at her elbow.

"Sorry," Poopsie whispered. She stuck her leg up in the air to match everyone else's.

Miss Adrienne seemed to take forever at the cassette player. Poopsie's leg was getting so tired, it wobbled in the air. She looked around. All the other legs looked a lot skinnier than hers; not one of them was wobbling. She stared up at the ceiling, switching quickly to her other leg.

Finally Miss Adrienne came back. "Flowers asleep," she said.

Poopsie opened one eye. Everyone else's legs were lowered. She let out her breath and put hers down too.

Her whole leg was pulsing.

Vi-sion, she told herself. Vi-sion of a just right leg that doesn't mind hanging up in the air by itself.

In about two seconds Miss Adrienne was saying, "Flowers awake."

With one eye on the girl next to her, Poopsie stuck her leg up in the air again.

She took a peek at Miss Adrienne too. Miss Adrienne was wearing a black leotard with pink tights and her hair was shiny black and hung down in one long braid to her waist. She also had on lots of blue eye shadow. Poopsie looked carefully but couldn't see Miss Adrienne's belly button through the leotard. Maybe she didn't have one.

"Point those toes," said Miss Adrienne. "Remember grace and beauty." Then she stopped. "What on earth are you doing here?"

Poopsie looked around. "You mean me?"

"Yes. How did you get in here?"

"My mother signed me up." She could feel everyone looking at her.

Miss Adrienne frowned a little, then smiled. "You're the beginner from High Flats?"

Poopsie bobbed her head up and down. She couldn't talk with everyone staring at her.

"Up you go," said Miss Adrienne, "into the next room. You don't belong with the advanced class."

"Oh." Poopsie heaved herself to her feet, trying to remember grace and beauty. She grabbed her ballet bag, tripped over the same girl's arm, and started for the door.

Behind her the girl muttered, "Don't you ever watch where you're going?" Everyone else began to giggle.

Poopsie reached for the doorknob.

"No, that's the bathroom," said Miss Adrienne, "it's the other way."

Her face red, Poopsie marched down the side of the room. "Flowers asleep," Miss Adrienne shouted again as Poopsie yanked open the door and slammed it behind her, shutting out the noise of the laughing.

She was in a room exactly like the other one, but there were fewer girls there and they were running around all over the place. "I'm Miss Adrienne," a voice called from the side near the windows.

Poopsie stood there wondering who the woman in the other room was. This Miss Adrienne was almost as pretty. Her hair was blond though, fluffy all over her head. She was wearing a pink-and-white leotard and matching pink tights.

She beckoned to Poopsie. "Come on, honey. Give me your name."

Poopsie took a breath. "Celeste Pomerantz."

"Lovely." She jotted Poopsie's name in a small notebook and clapped her hands. "Line up, girls," she said. "Today you are butterflies."

Poopsie looked around at the rest of the butterflies. One was fatter than she was. Poopsie closed her eyes for a minute. She couldn't believe it. She opened them again and looked at the girl's thighs. Jiggly.

It was a miracle.

She felt a sneeze beginning and groped in the shoulder of her leotard for some toilet paper. None there. Please don't, she told herself.

Aaah-choo.

She looked straight to the front, but from the corner of her eye she could see the girl next to her turning in her direction. She sniffled as quietly as she could. Too bad no one there had allergies, no one else had a nose like hers, a "Rudolph the Red-Nosed Reindeer" type.

"Wait till you hear about the great things we'll do this fall," said Miss Adrienne.

The butterflies picked up their heads.

Poopsie sniffled again, wondering how long she could go without a handkerchief. She tried to concentrate on what Miss Adrienne was telling them, something about raw carrots and broccoli. "Dancers need to be strong,"

It was a miracle.

PATRICIA REILLY GIFF

she was saying, "muscular . . . not soft like jelly doughnuts."

Poopsie took another look at the other jelly doughnut standing next to her. At the same time she tried to vision her nose to stop running.

WISH BOOK
Poopsie Pomerantz

In One Word, I Wish I Could Be:

Muskuler.

8

It was Wednesday, school was out early. "Caught you an autumn leaf," Poopsie told her mother as she opened the back door. "Butternut."

"Beautiful." Her mother reached for it. "I love that yellow color."

Poopsie picked an apple out of the glass bowl on the table. "I'm going upstairs right away. I want to practice ballet."

"Don't wake Teddy."

"Don't worry." She tiptoed up the stairs, hopping over the third step so it wouldn't creak, and went into her bedroom.

She looked around. It certainly wasn't a great place to practice dancing. The bed took up most of the room, with just enough space left for her dresser.

They were both disgusting. The bedspread used to be pink. Now it was almost white from all the washings. Sweet Pea, her doll, missing one eye and most of her hair, sat on the pillow hiding a blueberry jelly stain.

The dresser was worse. When she was five years old she had scratched her initials on the front of it with her mother's blue glass earrings. P for Poopsie, P for Pomerantz. Tracy Matson laughed hysterically whenever she saw it.

Poopsie pulled off her sneakers. She dropped the apple core in the corner, threw her school skirt and blouse on top of it, and changed into the green leotard.

She stared at the bedspread for a minute, then yanked it off. Angling the mirror over her dresser so she'd be able to see herself and Celeste at the same time, she jumped up on the bed.

She had to practice. She had to be perfect. Next week Miss Adrienne was picking parts for their first play, *The Ugly Duckling.* She had told them all about it, how the mother duck had hatched a swan egg by mistake, how different the little swan had looked, how unlike her own ducklings.

Poopsie put one arm over her head in a nice round curve, the way Miss Adrienne had said, and pointed the other arm at the mirror, where the audience would be. She wanted to try out for the part of the mother.

She stared at herself. The top half looked terrific, with her fingers nice and wavy and her arms curved just right. Her thighs were the problem. They jiggled even when she was standing still. She wouldn't even look at them.

She stood up on her toes for a bunch of bourrées, baby steps that Miss Adrienne called "boo rays." At least they sounded like that.

"Boo ray," she shouted, and baby-stepped down to the end of the bed. She bent her head a little to see better in the mirror, then gave a look of horror. She had just seen her son, the ugly duckling, for the first time. "Yeeks and ye gads," she yelled.

She had heard that on a pirate movie last week.

It sounded so great, she yelled it again.

In the next room Teddy started to scream, and outside she could hear a voice shout her name.

Tracy Matson. She probably wanted her to help clean the garage again. Poopsie clicked her teeth. They had worked on it every chance they had and still hadn't done half of it.

She jumped off the bed and bourréed over to the window to peek out behind the curtain. Maybe Tracy would go away. She wished Teddy would stop screeching like that, her mother would have a fit.

After a minute she heard her mother's footsteps on the stairs. She was probably in a ton of trouble for waking Teddy up. She made up her mind. She might as well go down to Tracy's. She waited until her mother had gone into Teddy's room. "I'm going over to Tracy's for a little while," she called as she pulled on her clothes.

"I wish you had thought of that sooner," her mother said.

Poopsie stopped in the kitchen and grabbed a carrot before she hurried out the front door and cut across Mrs. Clausson's lawn with Tracy.

"I thought we were going to work on the garage," Tracy said. "I've been waiting and waiting."

"I had to practice ballet."

Tracy snorted. "What's that thing . . . a carrot?"

"Want some?" Poopsie bit into it. "A little thick."

"Never mind thick," Tracy said. "You should have washed some of that dark stuff off." She threw open her garage doors. "I started without you today."

Poopsie looked around. She couldn't see one thing Tracy had done. The garage was still the worst mess Poopsie had ever seen. Cans of paint, old rope, a rusty metal swing, an orange plastic fish with one big eye. Boxes and rags littered the floor. She could hardly find room to put one foot down in front of the other. She sneezed and rubbed her nose.

"Over here," said Tracy. "Why don't you clean while I do the box. It'll be faster that way. We'll get a lot more done."

"Wait a minute, Tracy," Poopsie said. "My allergies are terrible in here. Look at all the dust." A fly zoomed around, landing on her head. "Yucks," she said, brushing at it. "See what I mean?"

"Flies are no problem," Tracy said. "No problem at all."

"They are to me. Disgusting things buzzing all over the place—"

"Look at the leaves outside," Tracy cut in. "Everything is turning red all over the place. It's getting cold. They're going to freeze themselves to death out there anyway."

"I guess so." Poopsie grabbed a couple of boards and moved them into a corner out of the way.

"Great," said Tracy. "Now just push that box over to the corner and we'll have a little open space for you to lie down."

"What do you mean lie down?" Poopsie asked. The cement floor was filthy. Dark oily marks dotted the center.

"I'll put some newspaper down first," Tracy said, "if you're so worried about getting dirty."

"But . . ."

"Don't you see? We have to measure the box. It has to be your size. No sense in building a box that's so small we can't even squish your stomach inside."

"Box?" Poopsie said. "You're still thinking about that? I thought you'd forgotten all about it. You bought the nails weeks ago."

Tracy put her hands on her hips. "I can't do every single thing at once," she said. "I've been practicing everything else, making quarters come out of people's ears and . . . never mind all that magic stuff now. I have to read that book again, figure out how to saw

71

without cut . . ." Her voice trailed off. "What are those two doing anyway?"

Poopsie swiveled around. Leroy and Richard were staggering slowly down High Flats Road carrying a long board on their shoulders.

Leroy was taller than Richard so the board was tilted at a crazy angle. They were laughing too. Poopsie watched them zigzag along, stopping every few steps to take a rest.

"Just the kind of a board I'm using for my sawing box," Tracy said. "Those copycats. They're probably doing the same thing. I knew I shouldn't have told them about it."

"Hey, Leroy," Poopsie called. "What have you—"

Tracy clamped a hand over her mouth. "Ssh. For Pete's sake, don't ask them that."

"I just want to find out," Poopsie mumbled.

Tracy took her hand away and wiped it on her jeans. "Let's sneak up on them, see where they're going."

Poopsie tiptoed down the driveway behind Tracy. Leroy and Richard were just disappearing down the side of the road. "They're going out alongside the bridge. On the rocks," Poopsie said.

"What would they want to do that for?"

"Want me to ask?"

"No," said Tracy. "I don't want you to ask. I want you to be quiet. We'll just kneel down on top of the bank, take a quick look over, and see what's going on."

Poopsie sank down in the weeds and popped her

head over the edge. Leroy and Richard were crouched on a rock jutting out into the river, the board lying next to them.

"Board's going to get wet," Tracy said. "Soaking wet."

Poopsie raised one shoulder. "Maybe they want it to get wet."

"Now that's the dumbest thing I ever heard." Tracy snorted. "But those are the dumbest two boys."

Poopsie sat back. She visioned herself bourréeing all over the place. If only she would get a good part in *The Ugly Duckling*. She knew she'd never get the lead, but wouldn't it be wonderful to be the swan's mother.

She opened her eyes, practicing her look of horror.

"Good grief," Tracy said. "What are you doing?"

"Nothing," said Poopsie. "Just working on my ballet stuff."

"Now that's another dumb thing. Look." Tracy pointed at the boys.

Leroy and Richard had stood up. They were pushing the board into the river. They watched as it floated away downstream.

"Now you can ask," Tracy said. "We'll never find out otherwise."

Poopsie cupped her hands around her mouth. "Hey, Leroy. What are you doing?"

They looked up. "What are you two doing? Spying on us?"

"Not me," said Tracy.

73

Tracy snorted. "Those are the dumbest two boys."

"Me neither," said Poopsie.

"You were so," Richard shouted. He and Leroy scrambled up on the rocks toward them.

Tracy and Poopsie raced down the road to the garage and sank down in front, panting. "Almost suppertime," Tracy said. "We certainly didn't get much done today. We'll work on it Saturday."

Poopsie shook her head. "I have ballet on Saturday."

"Skip it for one week. It won't make a bit of difference."

"We're going to pick parts for a ballet. If I'm not there, I won't be able to—"

Tracy cut in. "Able to get a great part?"

"I didn't say that exactly."

Tracy shook her head. "Don't get yourself all set up for this. You'll probably get a tiny part."

Poopsie looked at Tracy's face. She wished she could pop her right in the mouth. "Listen, Tracy. Everyone has a chance. And I'm going to practice for the rest of this week."

Tracy raised her eyebrows, then marched into the garage.

"Just wait," Poopsie said, almost to herself. Tracy wasn't paying attention. Tracy didn't believe she could get the part. Maybe she didn't even care.

WISH BOOK

Poopsie Pomerantz

If I Could Do Something Perfectly It Would Be:

These steps:

Tendu (Ton-do) Point with right foot.

*Relevé (Rela-vay) Up on toes.

Arabesque (A-ra-besk) Right foot forward – Left foot up and back.

9

On Saturday, Poopsie was late for her ballet lessons
again. She rushed down High Flats Road.

Tracy was outside her house, waving her Gypsy Wild
magic wand at Rebel. "Doesn't work, of course. My
luck."

"Can't talk," Poopsie said, breathless. "It's tryout day
at ballet."

"Didn't ask you to talk," Tracy said. "Just don't be
disappointed when it turns out you're not the lead."

Poopsie gritted her teeth. She was going to be the
swan's mother if it was the last thing she did. She had
practiced for about two hours last night. She did terrific
bourrées and her look of horror was wonderful. Even
her father had said so this morning at breakfast. He had
turned on the radio and she had begun to dance to the

music. She could feel the one-two-three, up-up-up beat to it, fast and twirly, and for a moment she had forgotten she was Poopsie. She felt like Celeste, swaying and moving exactly with the music.

Now she ran the last few steps to the bus stop. The bus was late too. At least she hoped it was late. She hoped it hadn't come and gone already.

Too bad she had overslept. Too bad one of her new ballet shoes had been missing. It had taken fifteen minutes to find it in the bathtub. Teddy was throwing everything he could find in there lately. If she hadn't been so late, she would have laughed to see the tub filled with toys and towels and everyone's underwear.

The bus had to be late. Everything was going wrong. Maybe it was because she couldn't get to sleep at night. She was worried, really worried about baby-sitting all alone in the house. Her mother was going to work next week. She walked up and down the road, shading her eyes with her hand, trying to see if the bus was coming.

Mrs. Clausson went by in her car, then Mrs. Wilson, with Leroy next to her. She was driving at about ten miles an hour. Mrs. Wilson had to be the slowest driver in High Flats, maybe in the whole county.

"Going to town?" she asked Poopsie, after stopping in the middle of the road.

Poopsie nodded. "I don't know what happened to the bus. I have ballet lessons at eleven o'clock. Miss Adrienne's Theater Ballet." She looked down the road again.

"Lovely," said Mrs. Wilson. "We're going right by there. Leroy has to have a dental checkup."

"Thank you, but I think I'd better wait for the bus," Poopsie said. If only she could see the bus coming down the road. It would take forever for Mrs. Wilson to get to Hancock.

"You'd be better off waiting for the bus," Leroy said in a muffled voice, his head almost covered by the sports magazine he was looking at. "My mother may not get there until midnight."

"Don't be silly, Leroy, open the door for her." Mrs. Wilson smiled at Poopsie. "We'd love to take you to town."

Poopsie glanced back down the road. Nothing was coming along but one of those big yellow cement trucks. "All right, I guess, if you don't mind." She climbed in. "Hi, Leroy," she said to the back of his head.

"Put that magazine down, for pity's sake," his mother told him. "Have some manners."

Leroy slapped the magazine down in his lap, but he didn't turn around. He just grunted.

"The trouble is," said Mrs. Wilson, looking into the rearview mirror at her, "Leroy's always eating junk food. And who knows when he brushed his teeth last. His toothbrush is always dry as a bone." She clicked her teeth about fourteen times. "He had eleven cavities last year. By the time he's thirty-five he'll have no teeth left, only fillings."

"He's not as bad as Richard," Poopsie said, trying to

be helpful. But Leroy just muttered something and slid down in his seat.

Behind them a horn beeped two or three times. Mrs. Wilson looked into the mirror. "Some people are so impatient."

Poopsie swiveled around. It was the bus trying to pass. Mrs. Wilson pulled over to the side and it sped past, leaving a trail of dust.

Poopsie sneezed.

"We'll just sit here a minute and let all that dust settle down," said Mrs. Wilson.

"No, don't worry. The dust doesn't bother me a bit. Not one bit." Poopsie sneezed again.

"I like that," Mrs. Wilson said. "You see how polite, Leroy. I'm sure she doesn't spend all her free time throwing wood into the river and telling her mother it's private business."

Poopsie leaned forward. "What was that about that wood, Leroy?"

"Better wait here for a little bit so I can see the road clearly," said Mrs. Wilson, almost to herself. "No good rushing and getting into some kind of accident."

"Told you to take the bus," Leroy said, staring straight ahead. "It'll get there today at least. We might as well be going across the desert. It'll be two weeks before we stagger in."

"It's all right," said Poopsie. "Do you know what time it is?" she asked Mrs. Wilson.

Mrs. Wilson looked at her watch. "Pretty close to eleven."

Poopsie sighed. She didn't want to be one minute late for the tryouts. She wanted Miss Adrienne to know she was dependable. Miss Adrienne wasn't going to give good parts out to just anybody.

"Your mother is very lucky to have you, Celeste," said Mrs. Wilson, starting up the car again.

Celeste. Poopsie felt a warm feeling in her chest. If only she were a Celeste. Thin and beautiful . . . and important enough for Tracy Matson to listen to once in a while. No one called her that except her teachers sometimes, her Aunt Barb, who was about ninety-five, and Mrs. Wilson.

"I wanted Leroy to take dancing lessons too," Mrs. Wilson went on.

Leroy muttered something.

"It certainly is not sissy stuff, Leroy," said his mother. "It would help you to be less clumsy. You might be able to navigate yourself through the dining room without bumping into every chair."

"There aren't any boys in my dancing class," Poopsie said to help Leroy out.

"Precisely. It's all this misinformation that ballet is only for girls," said Mrs. Wilson.

Leroy rolled his window down and stuck his head out. Poopsie sat back, practicing her looks of horror until she saw Mrs. Wilson staring at her in the rearview mirror.

"It is not sissy stuff, Leroy," said his mother.

Finally they reached Hancock. They passed the school and the church, then stopped at the stop sign to let about nine people cross the street. Poopsie held her ballet shoes bag in her arms ready to jump out of the car.

If only Mrs. Wilson would get there. She kept watching for the First National Bank clock to see how late it was.

At last they turned onto Main Street, Mrs. Wilson talking about dancing, and teeth, and all the money that dentists cost these days. Poopsie looked up. It was 11:30. Dancing lessons were half over.

She had her hand on the car door when the car stopped in front of Ronnie's Restaurant. She opened the door and got out. "Thanks, Mrs. Wilson, so long, Leroy," she yelled, slammed the door, and then dashed across the sidewalk and up the stairs, yanking off her shirt.

In the restaurant Ronnie must have been cooking cabbage. The front room upstairs, with the dark-haired Miss Adrienne and all the sleeping flowers, smelled terrible. Poopsie tiptoed through, trying not to notice that some of the flowers had raised their heads to see who was coming in so late.

She opened the door to her room. Everyone was leaning against a rail. "Sorry," Poopsie told Miss Adrienne. She sat down on the floor to pull off her jeans and toe into her ballet slippers, then she slid in behind the fat girl. She raised her leg a little to match the rest of the group.

Miss Adrienne smiled at them. "Pick up your feet," she said. "Pretend they're crayons, so you don't break them."

Tracy picked up her foot as high as she could. At the same time she leaned over and whispered, "Did Miss Adrienne pick parts yet?"

The girl covered her mouth with one hand and began to whisper something. She whispered a whole bunch of stuff. After every couple of words she blew a long strand of tan hair out of her eyes. Poopsie couldn't understand one word she was saying.

Up in front Miss Adrienne had clapped her hands. "Tendu," she yelled. "Point with your toe. Relevé. Up. High. Bourrée."

Everyone jumped away from the railing and raised up her arms.

"Tendu," Miss Adrienne said again.

Poopsie watched the girl next to her, but it wasn't much help. The girl didn't know what she was doing either. She kept saying "Wait a minute" and starting over.

They tendued, relevéd, and bourréed up and down the floor about a hundred times. Poopsie and the girl were about two feet behind the rest of the class. Every once in a while the two of them would stop dancing and run to catch up. Poopsie kept saying "Tondoo, rel a vay" under her breath.

84

She thought she'd drop right down on the floor. Her crayon legs and her feet felt as if they'd fall off. Up on the back wall the hands on the clock moved closer to twelve. Miss Adrienne still hadn't said one word about the Ugly Duckling.

At last she clapped her hands. "That's all for today, kids. Don't forget to bring your feathers next week."

Poopsie tapped the girl with the tan hair on the shoulder. "What about the Ugly Duckling?"

The girl picked her hair out of her mouth. "That's what I was telling you all this time. Don't you listen?"

"Sorry," Poopsie said.

"Sarah's the swan, of course. She's the best."

Poopsie nodded her head up and down a little. "I guess so. How about the mother?"

"Jessica's the mother."

"Oh," said Poopsie. "What about the rest of us?"

"I'm one of the regular ducklings," said the girl. "There are a lot of us. We have to bring feathers and wave them around while we dance." The girl sank down and took off her ballet slippers.

Poopsie sank down next to her. "What about me?" she asked after a minute.

The girl wound her hair around her finger, thinking. "You're one of the animals in the barnyard, I guess."

"What does that mean?"

"You're probably Porky. No one else wanted that part."

Poopsie's mouth felt dry. "What do I have to do?"

"Snort around. Stuff like that." She raised one shoulder. "We're going to practice next week."

Poopsie tied her sneaker laces and stood up. She went down the stairs slowly, reaching up her sleeve for her handkerchief. Then she started across the street. She made sure she kept her head down; she didn't want anyone to think she was crying.

Wait till Tracy Matson heard she was Porky, the barnyard pig.

10

Poopsie sat at the kitchen table chomping on a stalk of celery. It tasted good. Nice and juicy. What a week this had been. She'd been ducking around, staying out of Tracy's way since Saturday. In between she had tried to figure out whether she should quit ballet or beg Miss Adrienne for another part.

But tonight was the worst. It was Wednesday, the first night of her mother's new job.

Her mother was upstairs, wearing her best dress, her best shoes, and her best perfume. You'd think she was going to a party.

She didn't even care that she was leaving her two children alone in the dark for two hours. She didn't care that a kidnapper was probably camped out in Gypsy

Wild waiting to swoop down and capture them the minute she had pulled the car out of the driveway.

Her mother clicked into the kitchen. She had high heels on, the kind with just the big toes sticking out. The toes were painted Sweet Pea pink. She had borrowed the polish from Poopsie's doll, Sweet Pea. It was the only nail polish she could find in the whole house.

"Just stick the dinner dishes in the sink when you're done, lovey," her mother said. "Check on Teddy in his crib every once in a while. Daddy will be home by eight-thirty." She looked around. "That should take care of everything."

"The lock on the back door is broken," Poopsie said.

Her mother looked surprised. "It was broken when we bought the house. It probably will still be broken when we sell it."

"A kidnapper can walk right in here and take us out."

"He'll take one look at you and your brother, and he'll pick up his feet and run."

Poopsie kicked back and forth at the table rung. "That's not funny."

"Do you think I'd leave you if I thought you couldn't do this? You're growing up, you have to have some responsibility too." Her mother leaned over and gave her a hug. "You are safe, Poopsie, as safe as anything. Mrs. Wilson is next door, Mrs. Matson down the road, Mrs. Clausson—" She broke off. "If Teddy wakes up, he'll want a bottle. Just heat it up a little."

"On the stove?" Poopsie looked up, interested.

"No, not the stove, definitely not the stove. I don't want you near it."

"Then . . ."

"Run the hot water over the bottle . . . water from the fau . . ."

"I know." Poopsie put another celery stick in her mouth. "About that kidnapper," she said when she could talk. "Tracy thinks there really is one."

"Tracy's just trying to scare you."

Poopsie shook her head. "No. Really. Tracy is scared. I can tell."

Her mother shrugged into her jacket. "Use your head. What would a kidnapper be doing around here? And why would he stay here?" She looked up at the clock. "I can't believe the time."

Still shaking her head, she put Poopsie's dinner plate on the table, a hamburger with a slice of raw onion on top, a pile of dented peas, and some french fries, black on the ends.

"I hate this stuff," Poopsie said. "Why can't we have something good sometimes? Something like spaghetti?"

Her mother didn't answer. She went to the stairs and listened for a minute. "Good, he's asleep." She blew Poopsie a kiss and went out the door.

Poopsie went into the living room and looked at the television set. Better not turn it on, she thought. If a kidnapper was coming, she wanted to be able to hear him.

And there definitely was a kidnapper, Poopsie thought. Tracy, the toughest kid in High Flats, believed it. Maybe her mother and father believed it too. They were probably worried as anything. Maybe they figured they could get away with leaving their kids alone for a couple of hours. She pulled at a fingernail. Or maybe Tracy's father hadn't told them about the kidnapper at all.

Poopsie sat down again and looked at her dinner. Her mother had told every single person in town that she had a job. They all knew Poopsie was alone.

So might the kidnapper.

She picked up her fork, cut a piece of hamburger, and stared at it. Then she grabbed her plate and scraped everything off into the garbage. She put the dish and fork into the sink.

From the window she could see into the backyard. Everything was dark out there, almost black. There was a mist coming up from the river too. Just like on television. The kidnapper was probably creeping up, watching her from in back of the birch tree, waiting . . .

She yanked the shade down so hard, it snapped back and curled around the roller. It was too high to reach and pull down again. She stared at it for a minute, then sank down on the floor. She shoved at the kitchen table until it started to move. Then it slid across the floor easily. A moment later she crashed it into the back door.

That would keep the kidnapper out for about half a minute.

Upstairs, Teddy started to cry. That pest. She looked up. The poor pest didn't know he was going to be taken out of his bed any minute and dumped somewhere up in Gypsy Wild. Her mother and father didn't even have the money to pay the kidnapper. Teddy would be gone forever.

She tiptoed over to the window and peeked out again. There was a big lump of darkness over by the oak tree. She wondered what it was.

Once she had been on a train with her father, going to the dentist in the city. A man had sat across from them with long scritchy fingernails, pointy and dirty. She had hidden behind her father and peeked out to watch the man running his terrible fingernails through his hair.

The kidnapper probably looked just like him. Scritchy fingernails that would tap up and down the back door, coming around the side, lifting up the lock that didn't work.

She had to find a place to hide. A place for both of them. A good place the kidnapper would never find. She looked around. The broom closet?

Not an inch of room in there. There wasn't even room for the broom. It was filled with jars of tomatoes her mother had made during the summer, and apricot jelly from when Poopsie was in kindergarten. Nobody liked it, nobody ate it, but her mother said it was a crying shame and a waste to throw it out.

The hall closet. She could make a little tunnel behind the winter coats and boots and woolen hats.

She raced upstairs for Teddy. He was hanging half out of the crib, his undershirt stained with some kind of orange baby-food mush, screaming. He stopped when he saw her.

"All right," she said. "You're getting out of that crib now."

She hoisted him over the side, trying to keep her hands away from his wet diaper. "Let's go."

She hurried down the hall, bending backward. She wouldn't be able to carry him much more. He was heavy, really heavy.

"Shoom," he yelled, laughing, trying to hold on to the wall, slowing her down. "Shoom."

"Ssh." She tried to listen. Was the back door opening? Were nails scratching against the window?

She lumbered down the stairs and into the closet.

It was so black with the closet door closed, Poopsie couldn't even see Teddy's face.

The closet was as scary as the kidnapper.

Teddy didn't think so though. He was whispering "Shoom" and walking his fingers up and down Poopsie's face.

"Be very quiet," she whispered back. "Don't make a sound." She pulled a couple of boots around in front of them and sat back.

Teddy leaned back, too, against her legs. She didn't even mind his wetness. It was better than being alone in that closet, much better.

She sat there listening to his breathing. In, out, in, out, slower, slower. He was almost asleep. She felt a little sleepy now too.

Then she heard it. Definitely. Nails against a window. Scratching. Something at the back door. A thump. The table. Someone had pushed it back.

Teddy was heavy on her arm, sound asleep. How terrible if the kidnapper grabbed them. Worse if he grabbed Teddy. Poor little baby, he'd be so scared.

Another thump.

If she weren't such a Lily Liver, she'd get out of the closet, leave Teddy there. The kidnapper would take her, but he'd be safe.

Someone was in the kitchen now, walking around the table, rattling something, whistling.

Whistling.

She wanted to see, she had to see. If she could just open the door a slit, the tiniest little slit, she could look out and see those terrible nails, that horrible face.

She leaned forward and pushed at the door with one finger. A beam of light shone into the closet. She could see into the hall and the edge of the refrigerator in the kitchen.

She pushed again.

Tracy was sitting at the kitchen table, slathering a hamburger roll with ketchup.

93

Poopsie wanted to see, she had to see.

"Tracy Matson." Poopsie banged open the closet door. Next to her, Teddy slid over a little and rested his head against a pair of boots. She crawled out. "What are you doing here?"

Tracy took a huge bite of the roll. "No hamburger left?" She looked around. "What's the matter with your mother, keeping the table in such a funny spot? And what are you doing in the closet anyway?"

Poopsie swallowed. "Nothing. Looking for my sneakers."

"That's why I'm here, as a matter of fact. I need a pair of your shoes."

Poopsie raised one shoulder. "Can't find any extra. Teddy's been throwing my stuff in the tub, in the toilet, out the window. . . ."

Tracy rolled her eyes to the ceiling. "Glad he's not my brother."

"He's really cute sometimes, Tracy. He does funny things and—"

"I have a new trick. Excellent. I need a pack of cards or I'd show you right now. I wave my magic wand and I can tell you what card you have. Maybe it's a three or a queen or—" She broke off. "You should get that back-door lock fixed." She took another bite of roll. "I wouldn't stay in this house for one minute by myself."

Poopsie could hear Teddy in the closet. It sounded as if he was snoring a little.

What would Tracy think . . . the two of them hiding

in the closet? "Listen, Tracy, I've got to do homework now."

"You're not afraid here, all by yourself?"

"I have Teddy," Poopsie said, trying to move her chair back and forth in time with Teddy's snoring.

Tracy stood up. She raised one shoulder in the air. "I wouldn't waste too much time on homework. It's nothing but a big waste of time. Mrs. Fixx will go over the same thing a thousand times in the classroom. You'll know it like crazy by the time you get finished with her."

"I guess so," Poopsie said. Teddy was louder now. She stood up, too, and went over the sink. She turned on the water, loud.

"See you. Don't forget. Find those shoes as soon as you can. Bring them down to me." Tracy opened the back door and closed it behind her.

It wasn't until she had lugged Teddy out of the closet and back up to his crib that Poopsie stopped to think about the shoes. She should have asked Tracy why she wanted them.

She was just glad Tracy hadn't had time to ask about her part in the ballet.

11

It was Saturday again. The clock in Miss Adrienne's room pointed to 12:02. Everyone sank down on the floor to change back into sneakers. Everyone but Poopsie.

She waited for Miss Adrienne to turn off the cassette player, trying to think of what she could say about that barnyard pig business.

Finally Miss Adrienne turned around. Up close she looked different, nicer even. She had tiny freckles sprinkled on her nose and a dab of makeup on her chin. She smelled like flowers. Roses maybe. "Nice job today, Poopsie," she said. "I think you're going to be a dancer."

Poopsie swallowed. "I wanted to ask you. . . . Could I be something else?"

97

Miss Adrienne's forehead wrinkled. "I don't under-stand."

"I mean different from the barnyard pig." Poopsie looked away from Miss Adrienne's freckles and off to the side where Sarah the swan was shrugging into her jeans jacket. Sarah must weigh about forty pounds. Her neck was long and skinny and so were her legs. She almost looked like a swan.

"Everyone is going to laugh," Poopsie went on. "I'm kind of . . . I'm a little . . ." Poopsie came to a dead stop. How could she say her thighs jiggled like jelly? How could she say people might think she looked like a pig? Even Miss Adrienne might start to laugh. She looked away from Sandra and up at the clock. She was going to miss the bus back to High Flats.

"Different from the barnyard pig," Miss Adrienne repeated. "Sure." She patted Poopsie's shoulder. "We can always use an extra duck."

Poopsie took another breath. "Great. That settles it. I'll get some feathers like everyone else and—"

"The only thing is," Miss Adrienne said slowly, "there are a whole bunch of ducks, and only one pig. The pig gets to stand out. He roams around the barnyard danc-ing, twirling around. He's clumsy, but he isn't. He has to be a wonderful dancer. He makes everyone laugh."

"That's what I'm afraid of."

"Up to you," said Miss Adrienne. "Remember the point of being a dancer is to make other people feel the story."

"I guess so."

Miss Adrienne leaned forward. "You're worried that people will laugh at you? Not at the pig?"

Poopsie nodded.

Miss Adrienne nodded a little too. "I know what you mean, but don't you see, that's the thing about acting? The most wonderful dancers have played clowns and witches and—" She broke off. "You're acting. You're playing a part."

"I guess so," Poopsie said again. There was no way she was going to make the bus home now. It was probably halfway up the mountain. Her mother was going to have a fit if she had to get Teddy dressed and drive all the way down after her.

"Up to you though," said Miss Adrienne.

Poopsie sighed. "I guess so," she said for the third time. There was no way out of being a pig.

It was just one horrible day.

She pulled off her ballet shoes and toed into her sneakers. Then she went down the stairs slowly. She might as well take her time now. She had to go all the way over to Vinnie's Variety Store to use the telephone.

She shuffled through the leaves outside and started down the three blocks of Main Street looking in the store windows. After she passed the hardware store she crossed over to Vinnie's. Maybe if she had a little extra money in her pocket, she could get some chocolate or something.

Inside the variety store Tracy was standing at the candy counter. She was wearing a sweatshirt with a green alligator crawling across the front. The alligator's mouth was open in a wide grin so you could see his sharp yellow teeth.

"Where'd you get that neat shirt?" Poopsie asked.

Tracy raised one shoulder. "My mother's friend gave it to me. Her kid grew too much . . . can't wear it anymore. . . . Hey, what are you doing here?" She waved her hand at Poopsie's bag. "Never mind. I see the ballet slippers."

The counter woman moved toward them. "Did you make up your mind yet?"

"Uh-uh," Tracy said. "Still thinking."

The woman banged back to the other side of the counter, muttering about people who stood there for twenty minutes wasting time.

"I'm glad you're here," Tracy said. "I wanted to ask you . . ." She leaned forward, looking at the candy bins.

Poopsie closed her eyes. She knew what was coming next. The slippers had just reminded Tracy of that whole ballet business. Next she'd have something smart to say about Poopsie's getting the lead.

Poopsie felt her hands getting wet. How Tracy would laugh! What a great time she'd have telling everyone on the school bus about Lily Liver who was now a barnyard pig.

"Hey, what are you doing here?" Tracy asked.

Tracy leaned closer. "Actually I'm dying for some gummy bears, but I have about two cents in my pocket. Want to lend me a little?"

Poopsie took a breath. "Sure. Why not? I just have to save enough to call home for a ride."

"Don't worry. My father's over at the hardware store. We'll take you home." She ran her finger along the glass bins. "Miss?"

The woman didn't turn around.

Tracy tapped on the glass with her ring, a purple plastic skull.

"That's right," the woman said, turning around at last. "Break the glass, it's only been here since 1920."

"I'll take a pile of gummy bears," Tracy said, ignoring her.

"A pound? A half pound?"

"How much money you got?" she asked Poopsie.

"Two quarters."

"Two quarters' worth," she told the woman.

"Actually" —Tracy turned back to Poopsie— "I was going into the hardware store myself. I thought my father was going to get a haircut. I didn't know he was going to hang around looking at paint half the day." She clicked her teeth. "I need one last piece of wood for the box, but if I say one thing about it, everyone will be asking me what I'm doing, why I'm doing it—"

"How about making it one quarter's worth of gummy bears," Poopsie cut in, "and get something else too.

Those things stick to my teeth so hard, I can't even get my mouth open."

"You don't get enough for that." Tracy shook her head. "Besides, the lady put them on the scale already and she's got a very nasty temper."

The woman handed Tracy a little white bag.

"See what I mean? You could eat the bag and all in one gulp." She grinned. "If you don't want any, I can manage it myself." She held out the bag.

"Thanks a lot." Poopsie reached over and dug into the bag looking for an orange bear.

"I bought something else too." Tracy waved a brown bag in the air.

"What?"

"Socks."

Poopsie took a look inside at the pink plaid socks. "I have the same ones."

"Of course. That's the whole point. We need two pairs of the same socks. As soon as you give me the shoes, we stuff them inside."

"And . . ."

"It's a long story. I'll tell you some other time. Anyway, the box is almost finished," she said. They left Vinnie's and walked up Main Street toward the parking lot. "I just need that one little piece of wood and then you can pop yourself right in. There's our car."

Poopsie waved at Mr. Matson as he came toward them from the other direction. "I'm not being sawed in half. Not until you know what you're doing."

"Be quiet, will you? Want my father to hear?" She broke off when they reached the car. "How's ballet?"

Poopsie raised one shoulder as Mr. Matson smiled at her and opened the car door. She slid into the backseat next to Tracy. Mr. Matson got in the car and started it. They headed for home.

"Yeah," Tracy said, "what about ballet? Did you get a good part?"

Poopsie took a breath.

"I knew it," said Tracy.

"Knew what?"

"Knew you didn't get anything special. I said to myself they'd never let a kid like you—"

"As a matter of fact," Poopsie said, "I did get something good. I'm the ugly duckling, as a matter of fact."

"I don't believe it."

Poopsie moved her head up and down. Her mouth was dry. So what? Tracy would never see the ballet. It was a Saturday night down in town. She tucked the bag under her legs. "I even get to wear a feathered cap when he . . . when I . . . turn into a swan."

"I can't believe it," Tracy said again.

"Yes," Poopsie rushed on. "Miss Adrienne says I'm a dancer. She says my part is special."

"You have the best luck in the world," Tracy said slowly.

"I know." Poopsie watched the school slide past, and the church. A moment later they started up the mountain.

She didn't say another word the whole ride home. She just listened to Tracy talking about getting back at Leroy for something he had done last week. She hoped Tracy would never find out the truth.

WISH BOOK

Poopsie Pomerantz

I'd Like to Be:

Somebody else.

12

"Look at me," Tracy said. "Look exactly at me."

"I am." Poopsie tucked her chin deeper into the collar of her jacket. The last few weeks had been warm, but it was getting colder now. The wind blew across High Flats Road, sending swirls of dust and leaves into the air. Last week, on Halloween, they had had a few flurries of snow. Maybe it would snow again tonight.

Tracy stood on the bottom step in front of Poopsie's house. "Wait till you see this trick."

"I'm watching."

In back of them something banged on the storm door. Poopsie turned around to see Teddy, nose pressed to the glass, smiling a wet smile at her. His fingers were wet too. They made little round prints wherever he touched.

"What a mess that kid is," Tracy said.

Poopsie looked up at him. She could hear him going "Shoom, shoom" at her.

He did that every night when she baby-sat. She was trying to make him say Poopsie instead.

"Not such a mess, Tracy. He's just a little kid."

"Well anyway, are you watching?"

Poopsie settled back against the step. "Go ahead." It was going to be a great night tonight. Her father was off for the next two days. When it got dark they'd be laughing around the kitchen while he made his special frankfurters and cheese and told jokes.

The whole house would seem different, not dark and scary the way it was when she and Teddy were alone in the house.

Alone with a kidnapper outside.

"Are you paying attention?" Tracy asked. "I'm trying to show you this trick, and if you can't concentrate any better . . ."

"I can. I am. Don't worry."

"Then poke your two front fingers together over your nose and look at them," Tracy said, putting the tips of her own index fingers together in front of her nose.

Poopsie raised her fingers absently. It was a funny thing about baby-sitting for Teddy. He was getting cuter and cuter, not nearly the pest she had thought he was. The poor kid thought she was taking care of him, really taking care of him.

He didn't know about the dark and kidnappers. He thought she was like his mother.

"What do you see?" Tracy asked.

Poopsie jumped. "My fingers, of course."

Tracy put her hands on her hips. "You have them too close to your nose."

Poopsie moved her fingers out a little, staring around them at the birch tree that was dropping its last yellow leaves. How come it looked so scary at night, she wondered. During the day it looked regular, just an old tree, not big enough for anyone to hide behind. Not nearly big enough.

She'd have to remember that next time she baby-sat.

Tracy leaned over closer. "Move your fingers away from each other slowly. Then bring them back together again. Back and forth . . . back and forth."

Poopsie sighed. If only the back-door lock wasn't broken. It wouldn't be so bad looking out at that skinny birch tree. Maybe she'd be able to remember that it was too skinny for a kidnapper to hide behind.

"Well?"

Poopsie moved her fingers. "Hey," she said, "I have an extra finger."

"Told you. I read it right in the magic book." Tracy looked at her, beaming.

It was kind of a simple trick, Poopsie thought. Leroy and Richard might think so anyway. "Maybe you'd better get something more exciting," she told Tracy. "Leroy probably won't think . . ."

"What do you see?" Tracy asked.

Tracy tightened her lips and looked off toward the river. "You're right, I guess. Well, this trick was for warmers-up anyway. The main thing is the sawing box. Leroy will pay a pile of money when he hears I'm going to saw you right in half."

"If you think—"

"Now don't get all Lily Liver again. I've got the thing almost figured out. Going to make a fortune."

"That reminds me," Poopsie said. "What about the garage money? My part for cleaning up."

Tracy rubbed her hand across her mouth. "Spent it," she said. "I needed a decent can of paint. Why my father uses brown all the time I don't know." She narrowed her eyes. "I bought gold. A nice bright gold."

"With my money?"

"You'll get money from the magic show. Don't be so greedy."

Teddy was banging on the door with his block.

Poopsie turned around and waved at him to make him stop. "I really could use the money."

Tracy shrugged. "If you're going to be like that, I'll owe it to you." She stood up, dusting off the seat of her pants. "Here comes your father. It must be suppertime."

"When . . ."

"When what? You mean the money? After we do the sawing. I'll split it up right then and pay you. That minute if you like."

"It's just that I need it." Poopsie bit at her lip. "As

soon as my mother gets some money together, she's going to stop working and then I won't . . . Teddy won't . . ."

"You're afraid in the house," Tracy said. "I knew it. Old Lily Liver."

Poopsie didn't answer. Her father had pulled the car up on the driveway and was opening the door. He was grinning at them.

Tracy hopped off the steps and started down the path. "See you tomorrow."

At the same moment Poopsie's mother came to the front door. She looked great in Sweet Pea lipstick. "On my way," she said.

Poopsie and her father waved good-bye from inside the house, Teddy leaning against her legs. She picked him up and followed her father into the kitchen.

He reached down into a cabinet and brought out a pot. "I'm the best cook in the world, don't tell your mother. . . ."

Poopsie laughed. Her father was a terrible cook.

He stuck his head in the refrigerator. "Yes," he said, "I'm going to make something spectacular. Maybe some frozen corn and—"

The phone rang.

Poopsie put her hand on it.

"Pick it up, love," her father said. "Maybe it's a quiz show. Maybe we'll win a hundred dollars or so." He winked at her.

Poopsie took the phone off the hook and leaned against counter.

It was Tracy. "You been in my garage? Rooting around?"

Her father stuck a piece of celery in her mouth. "Uh-uh," she said as soon as she could talk. "Haven't been near it since I cleaned the whole thing with you. Never even got one cent for all that work."

"Someone's been here. Someone who was up at Gypsy Wild."

"One of the kids. Richard or someone."

"No. Nobody goes up there once it gets cold."

"But who . . ."

"You know who. Come down and take a look."

"I have to have dinner."

"After dinner."

Poopsie put the rest of the celery down on the counter. Her mouth felt dry. "It's dark after dinner."

"Gotta go," Tracy said. "My mother wants to use the phone."

"Wait a minute." But it was too late. Tracy had hung up.

"What was that all about?" her father asked, back toward her, chopping celery.

Poopsie opened her mouth. She wanted to talk about Gypsy Wild. She wanted to tell him what had been going on. She swallowed. "Why don't we get a lock that works on the back door?"

"You really worried about that?"

She nodded.

He looked over his shoulder. "I'll fix it for you."

Teddy fussed on her jeans. "That would be good," she said. She reached door and hugged the baby. Then she looked at the back door. Broken or fixed, it probably didn't matter. If a kidnapper wanted to get in, he could.

13

"Look at that." With one hand Poopsie rubbed at the window. With the other she tried to hold Teddy up high enough to see the snow. Great gobs of it were floating sideways across High Flats Road, covering the trees, the dried-up grass, and drifting over the ice on the river. The mailbox had a huge snow cap and so did her father's car.

"Shoom," Teddy said. "Shoom."

"Shoom is right." She smiled at him. The kitchen radio had just announced the snow news: no school today. If the snow kept coming down, maybe her father and mother wouldn't have to go to work tonight either.

"It's a holiday," she told Teddy, her face against his cheek.

It was going to be a real holiday. She wasn't going to

worry about a thing . . . not about being the barnyard pig . . . not about Tracy finding out . . . not about the kidnapper . . . and certainly not about what Tracy had found in her garage last week.

She shivered.

She could hear her mother beating eggs with a fork and smell bacon frying in the pan. Her mother was making French toast. She called it a snowstorm breakfast. Poopsie wandered in behind her father and hoisted Teddy into his high chair.

"What are you going to do with this perfect day?" her mother asked.

"Homework first, I guess." She reached into the cabinet for the box of corn flakes and dropped four or five on Teddy's tray. He loved them. "I have to do a composition. I can get it over with one-two-three and then I'm going to work on ballet."

"What's the composition?" her father asked, and at the same time her mother said, "You may sprout wings any day."

"Responsibility." Poopsie ducked her head. "I was supposed to do it Monday, but I forgot. Now I have to do fifty words instead of twenty-five."

Her father looked as if he were going to laugh.

"It's all Eddie's fault," she went on. "He wet a whole bunch of toilet paper in the bathroom, threw it on the ceiling, and it stuck. Then all the boys did it and the janitor says the boys' room ceiling looks as if it has clouds stuck to it."

Now her father did laugh. He leaned over her mother's shoulder. "I'm going to have eight slices of French toast, at least, I'm warning you." He smiled at Poopsie. "I'm glad to know you aren't making clouds on the bathroom ceiling."

"That's what Rita said in her composition, that she didn't even make one cloud and she shouldn't have to write the composition. Mrs. Fixx said she was very fresh."

"Don't say that then," said her mother, sliding a couple of pieces of French toast onto her plate.

Poopsie poured maple syrup and slathered it all over the top of her toast. "It's the watery kind so you need a lot."

"Certainly," said her father. He stood at the window yawning. "No sense in shoveling the snow yet," he said.

"Eight or nine inches?" Poopsie asked, swallowing a piece of bacon.

He smiled. "Two or three."

Her mother glanced out the window too. "Hope we can make it into Hancock to work tonight."

"Hope you can't," Poopsie said to herself.

"Suppose you heard there was a kidnapper here," Poopsie said, pushing the syrup bottle toward the middle of the table, not looking at either one of them.

"Are we back to kidnappers?" her mother asked.

Her father slid into the seat across from her. "I used to worry about kidnappers too," he said. "When I was your age."

"But suppose you saw something . . ."

"I did," her father said, and laughed. "Every night from my bed, I could see a kidnapper in the hall. The next morning he always turned into a coat rack."

Her mother laughed too.

"Shoom," said Teddy, blowing a damp corn flake into the air.

Poopsie leaned over her plate and ate quickly. The toast was wonderful, full of cinnamon and syrup. She wiped her mouth with her napkin, then went upstairs. Plopping herself down on the bed next to Sweet Pea, she tried to think of something to write. She didn't even have a decent pen. This one kept leaking black all over her fingers.

Everyone must have responsibility, she wrote. *You must have responsibility. It is important.*

She looked up at the mirror. Eleven words. She put in *very* before *important.*

This wasn't going one-two-three after all. It might take half the morning to get fifty words. She leaned over and reached under the bed for Sweet Pea's nail polish and painted a couple of her toenails. The polish was thick, gooey. It had been hanging around for as long as she had had Sweet Pea.

If you don't have responsibility, the boys' bathroom gets into a big mess. The girls' room can get in a mess too. Then the janitor has to clean too much. My teacher says responsibility is growing up.

Forty-nine words.

She wondered if Mrs. Fixx counted every word. She couldn't think of one more thing to say. Not one.

She wiggled her toes a little to be sure they were dry, then stood up. Last Saturday she had learned a couple of new steps for the next week's ballet. Humming a little to get herself started, she stood up on her toes and curved her arms over her head. It seemed as if Celeste were looking down at her.

"See that, Celeste," she said under her breath. "Relevé. Rel-a-vay."

She spun herself around, then stretched, jeté, jeté, and forward, left leg back and up, arabesque.

She twirled herself over to the window. Outside, the snow seemed to have lessened. She rubbed at the window, then pushed it up.

It was less. A lot less.

The snowplow was coming up the street, and Mr. Wilson had begun to clean off his car. And there was Tracy, a purple hat pulled down over her carroty hair, bent over almost double, shoveling her front path. She was working so fast, the snow flew up in a shower behind her.

Don't think about her, Poopsie told herself. Don't think about the kidnapper.

She started to dance again. She visioned herself up on the stage, the barnyard pig, dipping and spinning around. She was watching the ducks, snorting at the ugly duckling, following the mother around, feeling sorry for her poor ugly son.

Splat. A snowball smashed against the window. Tracy again.

Poopsie made believe she hadn't heard it. She sank down on the bed. Maybe she should think about the kidnapper, try to figure out what to do. She sat back, remembering that she had gone down to Tracy's garage the other day. At first all she saw was that it was a lot neater, a lot cleaner than it had been. That was because they had worked almost forever to get it looking right. In the middle were the oil stains, and almost covering them was the box Tracy was painting.

"See," Tracy had told her. "See."

"Nothing," Poopsie had said. "I don't see anything."

And then she had looked down to where Tracy was pointing.

A few drops of sticky red—something—were spattered across the floor next to the box. The same sticky red that had been spattered in front of Gypsy Wild.

"Could be anybody," Poopsie said, trying to swallow.

"Could be, but isn't."

"Your father's paint."

Tracy shook her head. "I told you he only uses brown."

Poopsie had shaken her head and backed out of the garage. Then she turned and raced for home.

Splat. She jumped. This time the snow hit the bottom of the still-opened window. Some of it landed inside on the floor, the rest on her responsibility paper. The blue lines smeared. What a pain that Tracy was.

She opened the window a little farther and stuck her head out. "Can't come out now," she called. "Have to do my homework over, all because of you."

She banged the window down again, not paying attention to what Tracy was saying, and reached for another sheet of loose-leaf.

14

It was Saturday, no ballet lessons because of the snow. Miss Adrienne would have a fit. She wanted to get in one last practice before the play.

"Go down to Mrs. Clausson, like a good girl," Poopsie's mother said. "I need a good recipe for fish soup. I'll cook it today, and we'll have it for Sunday dinner."

Poopsie gagged. "I can't stand fish."

"Your father loves it."

Poopsie pulled on her boots and stamped down High Flats Road. She didn't even look at the recipe Mrs. Clausson handed her out the front door, and barely listened as she went on about it being the best soup in the world.

As she started back Tracy popped her head out her

front door. "Where are those shoes anyway?" she called.

"Forgot again, sorry."

"Come take a look in here." Clutching her sweater around her, Tracy sped down the driveway and yanked the garage doors open.

Poopsie followed her, feeling the palms of her hands turning wet. All she could think of were the stains, thick and red, on the floor. She had thought of them for days now, worried about them.

Tracy pointed to the box, held together with huge nails, painted with a gold paint as thick as Sweet Pea's nail polish.

"Don't you see," said Tracy, "the whole thing of the box is that you squinch up in one half, and we stick a pair of your shoes on a stick out the other. Then zippo. Saw right down the middle."

"I guess so," Poopsie said. The box looked as if it would fall apart any minute.

"Not only that," said Tracy, "we'll drip a little ketchup through this knothole. Richard and Leroy will be trying to figure it out for the next fifty years."

"I'm baby-sitting for Teddy tonight," Poopsie said, trying not to look at the red stains next to the box.

Tracy raised one shoulder.

"It's my mother and father's anniversary. My father asked me to do it for them." She bit at her lip, remembering her father dancing her mother around the kitchen. "We'll go to La Salette," he said. "Have dinner, dance." Her mother had been smiling, laughing. . . .

"So . . ." Tracy said.

"If the kidnapper comes back, if he finds out there are two kids alone in a house . . ."

"With the back-door lock broken," Tracy added.

Poopsie shook her head. "No, my father fixed it for me."

Tracy looked down at the box. "It's still scary."

"That's why we have to go down there," Poopsie said.

"Go down where?"

"To Gypsy Wild. I have to find out about that kidnapper. I have to see if something's there."

"You're crazy."

"I keep thinking about Teddy. I keep thinking about me too."

"The river's frozen, you can't take the boat."

"Walk," Poopsie said, tightening her mouth.

"It's too cold."

"We'll wear a million scarves."

"Count me out." Tracy scrubbed at the floor with an old rag, scrubbing at the red stains.

"Count you in," Poopsie said. "You're not afraid of anything."

Tracy didn't answer.

"Tracy?"

"All right, this time I'm afraid." She wiped her hands with the rag.

Poopsie didn't say anything.

"Suppose there really is a kidnapper up there?"
Tracy asked.

"We'll take a baseball bat, just in case." Poopsie swallowed. "But we won't go near him. We'll take a quick
look, make sure he's there, then go down and call the
police."

"We could bring Leroy Wilson." Tracy tried to grin.
"Send him first. If the kidnapper grabs him, we'll run
for help."

Poopsie started to laugh, thinking about Leroy racing
away from the kidnapper.

Then Tracy sighed. "When do you want to do this?"

"Right now. Right this minute, before I lose my cour-
age."

"I thought so," Tracy said. "Hang on."

Poopsie waited by the garage door, shivering while
Tracy dashed into the house. The sky was still gray with
snow, and it looked as if a few flakes were drifting down
again.

A moment later Tracy came out, bundled into a wool
jacket, and handed her a long plaid scarf and a pair of
fuzzy earmuffs. "Shall we really get Leroy?"

Poopsie shook her head. "He'll never do it anyway."

They headed for the river and a few moments later
stood on the riverbank. The reeds had fallen over in
frozen piles. "Easier to get down," Poopsie said as she
slid between them and hit the ice on the river.

The river was frozen so solid under a thick cap of
snow that Mr. Clausson could have driven over it with

"Shall we really get Leroy?" Tracy asked.

his tractor. Dozens of footprints zigzagged from one side to the other. The ice fishermen must have been out yesterday. It was hard walking. After a few minutes Poopsie's legs began to ache.

"Cold," Tracy said, gritting her teeth.

"Freezing." Poopsie put her mittens up to her stinging cheeks.

It seemed forever until they reached the pine trees on the other side of the river near Gypsy Wild. There the snow seemed deeper. "Harder to run if we have to." Tracy whacked a branch with her baseball bat.

"I could go first." Poopsie felt her heart beat under her jacket. "You wait here. If I yell, get help." She tried to smile. "I don't mean Leroy. I mean Mr. Clausson, or somebody like that."

Tracy stared at her. "You swallow brave pills or something?"

Poopsie shook her head. "I'm so scared, my knees are shaking. But you know what, Tracy? I'm sick of being afraid all the time." She sniffed a little. "And you know what else? I'm worried about Teddy. Suppose something happened to him? He's so little."

"You think I'm going to let you go up there alone?" Tracy waved the baseball bat around. "Ruin my reputation? Have that nut-case Leroy find out and laugh all over the place? You think I want to be called Lily Liver?" She pointed the bat at Poopsie's nose. "You wait here."

Poopsie sighed. She'd love to wait behind the trees.

She'd sink right down in the snow, pull herself into a ball under the big pine tree, and hide. "No, I'm coming."

They marched together through the trees until they reached the clearing and the cabin. The windows were blank, no lights, no curtains. The door was slightly open.

They moved back behind the trees. Poopsie could hear herself breathing, could see the white smoke puffing out of her mouth.

"Look," Tracy clutched her arm. "Someone's in there."

For a moment they didn't move. Through the opened door Poopsie could see the end of a couch, the stuffing coming out of the arm, an old gray couch that the kidnapper probably sat on at night thinking about the children he was going to capture. Horrible.

"Run," Tracy yelled.

They dashed through the trees, around the rocks, and didn't stop until they were almost back to the river.

Poopsie grabbed hold of Tracy. "Wait." She was so breathless, she could hardly get the word out.

"Don't wait."

"Yes, wait." Poopsie tried to get her breath. "How do you know someone's in there?"

"I could see. Someone's behind the window. Something moved."

"Let's go back." Poopsie's teeth were chattering. "Take a quick look, to be sure."

They stared at each other. "All right," Tracy said, "We'll just go up to the edge of the trees and watch."

"Right."

They went back slowly, ready to run if they saw anyone or heard anything, almost tiptoeing through the snow. Then Poopsie pointed down. She could see footprints now, leading right up to the open door. "More than one person," she whispered. "Two different kinds of boots."

"Not all that big," Tracy said slowly. She put her foot in one of the prints. "See what I mean?"

Poopsie looked up at the window. Something was moving inside.

"Kids." Tracy drew in her breath. She sounded furious.

Poopsie squinted down at a print. "Kids?"

"Look," Tracy said. "This boot is hardly bigger than mine. Maybe an inch."

"A small man. A woman," Poopsie said, but she knew it wasn't true.

They marched up to the door of Gypsy Wild, their feet crunching in the snow now, their steps loud on the three steps to the top.

The door opened the rest of the way, showing a slice of red wall behind the couch, a football poster, and then a foot.

"Leroy Wilson," said Tracy. "It's Leroy, that weasel."

Richard popped his head out around Leroy. "Get out of here," he said. "This is a private club."

Poopsie stepped back. She couldn't believe it.

Leroy and Richard.

She had worried all this time for nothing.

She picked up a fistful of snow in her mitten and tossed it at them as hard as she could.

The snowball spattered on Leroy's shoulder and landed on the cabin floor.

"Run," Tracy yelled.

They took off through the trees and ran all the way to the river. "Did you see that?" Tracy asked. "The living-room walls? All uneven and painted the ugliest red you ever saw."

"Bloodred," said Poopsie, laughing. "And that's why they were floating boards down the river . . . for their walls."

She closed her eyes. "I can't wait to get home. I can't wait to baby-sit for my mother and father tonight. The door will be locked, and Teddy and me inside . . . no kidnappers behind the birch tree." She took a deep breath. "Let's go."

"Right," said Tracy. "My mother might even let me come down and keep you company."

For a while they walked along the frozen river without talking. The sun had gone down, it was getting dark. Poopsie scooped up a clump of snow and threw it at a rock. Next to her, Tracy grinned. "That reminds me. I told my mother about your taking ballet lessons and being the star in the show."

"Really?" Poopsie said, her mouth suddenly dry.

"She's going to get my father to take me to it. Look the whole thing over, watch you be the ugly duckling. Maybe I'll even take lessons myself."

Poopsie bit her lip, trying to think of what to say. "I don't think you'd really want to come," she said. "Just a bunch of kids dancing around, you know. Just a—"

"Don't be ridiculous," Tracy said. "I know it won't be so hot. But with you in the lead" —she smiled at Poopsie again— "you know, I'll bet you're pretty good."

Poopsie swallowed.

"So it's settled. I'm coming."

Poopsie scuffled her feet in the snow. She opened her mouth to tell Tracy the truth, but she just couldn't seem to get the words out.

WISH BOOK

Poopsie Pomerantz

I'm Going to Try to:

Stop lying.

15

Tonight was the night of the ballet, the night Tracy was going to find out Poopsie wasn't the star, that she had the silliest part in the whole show. But this afternoon they were going to pay Leroy and Richard back for that kidnapper business. Poopsie crossed her fingers. Maybe.

She pulled on her jacket, opened the door, and hurried down High Flats Road to Tracy's garage. Inside, nine old kitchen chairs with paint flaking off were lined up in a row. Poopsie almost laughed. "Where do you think you're going to find nine people for an audience?"

Tracy waved a hand in the air. Poopsie could see she was wearing nail polish. She looked excited. "Just to make it look authentic, you know, like a real theater."

Poopsie sank down in one of the chairs and looked up at the tan curtain Tracy had looped over a wash line. There was a huge rip down the center that Tracy had tried to sew with black thread. She hadn't done a very good job. Through the spaces it was easy to see the edge of the gold sawing box.

"Too bad it's a little cold for your green leotard," Tracy said.

Poopsie was glad it was cold. She could just imagine Leroy and Richard laughing all over the place at her.

"Are you ready?" Tracy pointed. "Here they come."

The boys trudged down the driveway toward them. "What's the matter with you," Leroy said, "calling my mother and asking her to send me down here right away. Are you crazy?"

"Yes, they're crazy," Richard said. "Look at that coffin sticking out."

Tracy waved her hands again, flashing red nail polish. "In one moment the curtain will open and you will have the chance . . ." She stopped for a breath. "A chance to see the magic of a girl being sawed in two. Yes, I said sawed in—"

Leroy peered around the curtain. "That's going to break the minute you lean on it."

That was true, Poopsie thought. The whole thing was crooked and wobbly and out of line.

"One buck to see Poopsie sawed in half," Tracy said. "Guts coming out and everything."

"You are crazy."

"You, too, Richard. One buck."

Poopsie leaned back against the wall. If only they could have practiced. But Tracy had laughed at her. "Once we saw this box in half, it's ruined. Finished. Kaput, as they say on TV."

"No dollar, no sawing," Tracy was telling the boys.

Leroy had one hand in his pocket.

Poopsie could see Tracy grinning. He was about to pull out the money. Richard was eyeing the box, trying to decide if it was worth it to see Poopsie Pomerantz cut in half.

It was. He handed a crumpled-up dollar bill to Tracy. So did Leroy. She put them on a chair.

"Ta da," Tracy said. She picked up the saw. "The great Master Matson will now start the show." She raised the top of the box a crack and waved to Poopsie to get inside.

Poopsie climbed into the box carefully. Good thing she was taking ballet lessons. She kept repeating "Grace and beauty" as she slid inside, smiling until Tracy slammed the top of the box down over her head.

The box shook as if it would fly apart.

It was dark inside. Poopsie had to reach around to find the extra pair of shoes with the pink plaid socks stuffed inside them.

"Stick your feet out the end of the box," Tracy was yelling, as if Poopsie were a million miles away.

She couldn't find them. They must be way down at

the end. She tried to wiggle down a little, but the box started to shake again.

"Poopsie Pomerantz will now put her feet out of the end of the box," Tracy shouted.

"Hold your horses," Poopsie said. She gave one last lunge toward the end of the box and put her hands on the sticks that were jutting out the end of the shoes.

"POOPSIE POMERANTZ WILL NOW STICK HER FEET . . ."

Poopsie shoved the shoes on sticks outside the box.

"Now," said Tracy. "I will use this saw, sharp as a razor, sharp as a sword. I will cut Poopsie Pomerantz exactly in half."

"There's got to be a trick to this," Richard said.

"No trick at all," said Tracy. "It's magic. Magic I've studied from the East, from—"

"From that book you won at Tracy's birthday party."

Poopsie could hear Tracy begin to saw. She could feel the box shaking too. She pulled her legs up against her stomach as hard as she could, making a tight ball. The bottle of ketchup dug into her side. It was a good thing it was wintertime, she thought. It was getting a little warm in the box.

"Is this going to take all day?" she could hear Richard saying. "We've got to get down to our club and finish all that painting."

Richard was right, Poopsie thought. It was taking a long time.

"Is it beginning to hurt?" Tracy asked.

"Is this going to take all day?" Richard asked.

"Aheeee," Poopsie yelled. She had almost forgotten to scream.

"Thought so," said Tracy.

"Help," Poopsie said.

Just then she could see the edge of the saw coming through the wood above her. She opened the top of the ketchup bottle and squeezed it. Good. The ketchup was ready.

The saw was digging into the side of the box now. Poopsie got ready to squeeze the ketchup through the hole. The box started to shake. She held out her hand to steady herself.

The next thing she knew she had landed on the garage floor in a pile of wood. The box had fallen apart. Leroy and Richard were looking down at her, doubled over with laughter, pointing. She had ketchup down the front of her jacket and a blob of it across her jeans.

Before Tracy could stop them the boys had grabbed the two dollars and were racing down the driveway. Tracy stood there, the saw in her hand, sawdust sprinkled over her sneakers.

"What happened?" Poopsie stood up gingerly.

Tracy didn't answer. She bit her lip, staring down at the pieces of wood.

Poopsie reached for a rag and wiped at the ketchup. Was Tracy going to cry? she wondered. It certainly looked like it. She put her hand on Tracy's arm.

"I don't care," Tracy said. "I don't care two bits about the old sawing box."

"What happened?" Poopsie asked again.

Tracy shook her head. "I don't know exactly. But I just remembered all that sticky red stuff on the floor. It was from Leroy and Richard's paint. They probably knew about the whole thing. Sawed through part of the box. Who knows?"

"Those weasels," Poopsie said. "We'll get back at them some other time."

Tracy raised her shoulder.

"I'm sorry," Poopsie said. "I'm really sorry."

Tracy was crying. She could see it now. Her eyes were watery, her chin quivering. Poopsie couldn't get over it. Tracy Matson, the toughest kid in town, crying. "We'll try it again," she said. "We'll try another trick."

But Tracy had turned around and was running up the driveway.

Poopsie watched her run into the house and slam the door. Poopsie bent down to wipe up the ketchup on the garage floor. For a moment she wanted to run after her. What could she say though? The only thing she could think of was telling her about being the barnyard pig.

She scrubbed at the ketchup. She couldn't tell her that, never. Tracy would laugh and laugh. She sighed and stood up. It was time to go home, time to eat Mrs. Clausson's horrible fish soup. And almost time to be Porky, the barnyard pig.

PATRICIA REILLY GIFF

WISH BOOK

Poopsie Pomerantz

The Best Thing ~~Would Be~~ <u>was</u>:

Telling my mother the whole kidnapper story.

16

Poopsie could hardly breathe. She could hardly see either. Miss Adrienne had just plopped a huge papier-mâché pig head down over her hair. Her mother had spent an hour on her hair after dinner, making neat curling-iron curls. Now they were ruined.

She went over to look in Miss Adrienne's full-length mirror. Next to her stood Sarah, the ugly duckling who would turn into a swan. You couldn't see her hair either. All you could see was a gorgeous feathered hat with diamonds all over it. Lucky Sarah.

One good thing, she thought, no one would ever know it was old Poopsie under that pig head. It was so big, it made the rest of her look almost skinny. She ran her hand over her stomach. She could hardly see her belly button sticking out of the pale green leotard.

Maybe it was all that celery and carrots she'd been eating instead of potato chips.

She squinted at the head again. Bright bubble-gum pink. Little stick-up ears. A pushed-out snout. No one would ever know—not even Tracy Matson.

Perfect. She'd skip right out into the audience after the show, tell Tracy she'd been sick to her stomach, had a headache, a temperature, 102, something like that. She'd say she had to lie on a couch in the back of the stage, and at the last minute Sarah had volunteered to be the ugly duckling. Of course she wasn't as good as Poopsie, but what could you do? Sick was sick, and the show had to go on.

Miss Adrienne clapped her hands. "Into your places, everyone."

Poopsie straightened her pig head and hurried to the back of the stage.

"Ready?" asked Miss Adrienne.

Everyone nodded. A moment later the red velvet curtain jerked open and the audience began to clap. Her mother and father were in the first row, with Teddy crawling on the floor in front of them. On an end seat toward the middle was Mrs. Fixx.

Her teacher, Mrs. Fixx. Poopsie couldn't believe it. She hadn't even seemed to be paying attention when Poopsie told her about the ballet last week. It was a good thing she had told Mrs. Fixx the truth, that she had said she was only the barnyard pig. Mrs. Fixx would have found her out even behind that papier-mâché mask. Mrs. Fixx found everything out sooner or later.

A bunch of other people were in the audience too. Parents, Mr. Bassin from the drugstore, Mrs. Walker from Frozen Yogurt, Mrs. Wilson, and there was Tracy sitting on her feet in the back. Poopsie wouldn't look at Tracy though. She wouldn't think about her.

And then it was time to begin. The ugly duckling's mother danced around her babies, a couple of ducks, and the ugly one, a brown paper hat hiding the feathered one underneath. Poopsie moved out behind the mother, relevé, relevé, relevé. Her hands felt damp, her feet were stiff.

The mother threw up her arms in horror. Poopsie looked over her shoulder to see what was the matter, jetéd back, arms up, grunted. Poor mother, horrible baby.

The audience loved it. They began to clap.

Poopsie arabesqued around, clumsily, as Miss Adrienne had said, the way a pig would dance. She shook her big head over the poor mother's troubles. She could feel herself loosen up. Instead of being nervous, she began to enjoy the dancing. After all, Tracy would never know.

In front, Teddy was pointing up at her. "Shoom," he said, smiling a big wet smile, his two new top teeth showing.

She arabesqued a little closer. He was waving at her, even though he didn't know who she was.

She waved back. A couple of people in the audience laughed, and Miss Adrienne would have a fit if she knew it, but Poopsie was glad she had done it anyway. He looked so happy. She wondered why she had thought he was such a pest last summer.

It was fun to dance with the pig head on. She felt like someone else, almost like Celeste, dancing around, making everyone smile.

She took a quick peek at Tracy. Tracy was sitting up a little higher. Maybe she was looking for her. Yes, now she was shading her eyes with her hand, getting out of her seat, standing on tiptoes. Too bad.

Poopsie twirled around and watched the ugly duckling. He wandered around the barnyard alone while the other ducklings danced behind their mother. Poopsie could feel his sadness. Sarah was doing a wonderful job. Even when the ugly duckling followed his mother and the other ducks onto the pond Miss Adrienne had made out of an old mirror, they glided away from him. Poopsie shook her huge head and danced around the pond. It was an important dance. Everyone else was hardly moving. They were watching her feel sorry for the poor lonely duckling.

The curtain came down. The first act was over. Poopsie listened to the clapping outside, raising the pig head a second to rub her neck and chin.

"See, Poopsie, what did I tell you?" Miss Adrienne whispered. "Only one pig. Lovely dancing."

The curtain went up again. Poopsie was having a

wonderful time. So was Tracy. She could see her laughing when she was supposed to laugh, looking sad when the ugly duckling was left alone with only his old friend the pig to cheer him on.

Tracy wasn't as tough as Poopsie had thought she was. She wasn't as mean either. Poor Tracy. Too bad that sawing box hadn't worked out right. Leroy and Richard always seemed to win.

Poopsie danced around the lonely duckling, thinking about Tracy. She was turning out to be a friend, maybe.

It was time for the climax. Sarah, the ugly duckling, bent her head as if she were looking into the pond. Poopsie stepped forward, moving her head slowly, watching. She reached out and lifted the brown paper hat off Sarah's head and let it drop on the stage. Sarah's feathered hat sparkled under the lights. She was beautiful, a swan. She bourréed onto the pond and did a graceful dance.

A moment later the ballet was over, with everyone in the audience clapping, and behind the curtain everyone hugging each other.

"Bravo," Miss Adrienne kept saying. "Bravo."

They stood in a line, ready for the curtain call. "Take off your pig's head, Poopsie," Miss Adrienne whispered from the side. "Let everyone see who you are."

Poopsie shook her head no. The curtain opened. Everyone kept clapping as the dancers bowed, everyone except Teddy, who was asleep, head back, mouth open, on her father's arm.

The curtain closed and opened again. The dancers gave one last bow and it was over.

Poopsie pulled off the pig head and gave it back to Miss Adrienne. She threw her clothes on over her leotard and went outside to her mother and father.

Mrs. Wilson and Mrs. Fixx were standing next to them. "Such talent," Mrs. Wilson was saying. "That Celeste is a lovely girl."

Poopsie stood up on tiptoe a little, trying not to let them see she was looking around for Tracy.

"She's turning into a young lady," said Mrs. Fixx. "I take some credit for that."

"Shoom," Teddy said over his father's shoulder.

Tracy was coming up the aisle toward her.

"Excuse me," Poopsie said quickly. All she needed was for Mrs. Wilson or Mrs. Fixx to say something about her pig part.

She ran to meet Tracy halfway down the aisle. "I'm feeling a little better," she said before Tracy could open her mouth. "Not so dizzy. I guess I'm going to be all right."

"You look all right to me," Tracy said.

"I was feeling so sick, I had to lie down on the couch. It was a good thing that Sarah—"

"Sarah was okay," Tracy said. "A little wobbly."

"Well—"

"But you—"

"At the last minute I had such a stomachache that Miss Adrienne said I'd better not—"

Sarah's feathered hat sparkled under the lights.

PATRICIA REILLY GIFF

"You were the best."

Poopsie looked back at her mother, who was smiling at Mrs. Fixx and nodding. "Me?"

"I guess you know that anyway," Tracy said.

"But . . ." Poopsie began and stopped. Then she leaned forward. "Pretty silly to be the pig."

"Best part in the whole thing. You can't be a Lily Liver to stand up in front of the whole world as a big pink pig."

"That's kind of what Miss Adrienne said." Poopsie stood up on her toes. "You know, Tracy," she said, "I just love ballet."

"It's not bad," Tracy said, nodding. "Think I'm going to join myself. You can show me some stuff."

Poopsie nodded.

"Maybe we can even borrow that pig's head, play a great trick on Leroy and Richard."

They looked at each other and laughed. "Only if you promise something," Poopsie said.

Tracy did a little relevé in the aisle. Not a very good one, but not bad either. "Okay. What?"

"How about," said Poopsie, "calling me Celeste?"

WISH BOOK

Poopsie Pomerantz

I Wish:

Every night could be like this... the ballet, having Tracy for a friend, and best of all my mother telling me I'm growing up! That's good, she says, because we're going to have another baby next summer. I hope he's just like Teddy.

About the Author

Patricia Reilly Giff's earlier books about Casey, Tracy, and Company are *Love, From the Fifth-Grade Celebrity; Fourth-Grade Celebrity; The Girl Who Knew It All; Left-Handed Shortstop; The Winter Worm Business;* and *Rat Teeth*. She is also the author of the Kids of the Polk Street School books, the Polka Dot Private Eye books, *The Gift of the Pirate Queen,* and the popular mysteries featuring Abby Jones, Junior Detective— *Have You Seen Hyacinth Macaw?; Loretta P. Sweeny, Where Are You?,* and *Tootsie Tanner, Why Don't You Talk?*

Patricia Reilly Giff lives in Weston, Connecticut.

About the Illustrator

Leslie Morrill has illustrated all Patricia Reilly Giff's books about Casey Valentine and her friends. He lives in Madison, Connecticut.